Ranya O. Khalifa has had a lifelong passion for writing and story-telling since the age of eight, holding a strong unshakeable belief that the written word is a majestic tool whereby an author imprints images in every reader's mind. Her poetry collection, entitled, *'To the Majesty of the Word'*, attests to her fundamental conviction that words are extremely powerful and potent means of human story-telling and emotional connectivity.

This is her second thriller novel, yet the first in the murder-crime sub-genre, where she takes the reader on a no holds barred 'who-dun-it' high speed-chase. Full of explosive twists and turns, multiple villains, and a slew of con artists, readers should expect nothing less than a breathless, unstoppable rollercoaster ride.

Ranya holds a B.A in mass communication and an M.A in middle eastern studies from The American University in Cairo, Egypt. She has worked in several fields such as journalism, advertising, research, and has had a lifelong passion for traveling, poetry writing, as well as performing and visual arts.

This book is dedicated to my two children, Nadine and Rasheed, as well as to my supportive husband, without whom my second thriller novel would have never come to be.

In memory of my beloved father:
Daddy, I know you are smiling with pride in heaven...

Ranya O. Khalifa

SUITE 55

AUSTIN MACAULEY PUBLISHERS™
LONDON * CAMBRIDGE * NEW YORK * SHARJAH

Copyright © Ranya O. Khalifa 2023

The right of Ranya O. Khalifa to be identified as author of this work has been asserted by the author in accordance with Federal Law No. (7) of UAE, Year 2002, Concerning Copyrights and Neighboring Rights.

All rights reserved. No part of this publication may be reproduced, stored in a retrieval system, or transmitted in any form or by any means, electronic, mechanical, photocopying, recording, or otherwise, without the prior permission of the publishers.

Any person who commits any unauthorized act in relation to this publication may be liable to legal prosecution and civil claims for damages.

The age group that matches the content of the books has been classified according to the age classification system issued by the Ministry of Culture and Youth.

ISBN – 9789948779704 – (Paperback)
ISBN – 9789948779711 – (E-Book)

Application Number: MC-10-01-4130346
Age Classification: 17+

Printer Name: iPrint Global Ltd
Printer Address: Witchford, England

First Published 2023
AUSTIN MACAULEY PUBLISHERS FZE
Sharjah Publishing City
P.O Box [519201]
Sharjah, UAE
www.austinmacauley.ae
+971 655 95 202

I would like to acknowledge all the sacrifices that the police, drug law enforcement officers, and national security personnel undertake in order to keep citizens safe.

Your sacrifices will never be forgotten.

Chapter One
'36 Hours Ago'

After a tormenting sleepless night, Mona finally received a text message on her phone. She was instructed to go to the Imperial Hotel at exactly nine o'clock that night. She was to go directly to the Maharaja Indian restaurant, where she would order an entree and then discreetly hand over her flash drive to the maître D' before exiting the restaurant.

Mona wasn't sure if anyone would believe the evidence she had painstakingly gathered over the past eight months. She had worked almost every contact she had made throughout her two decade journalistic career, probing countless leads and carefully extracting the information she needed to piece together this explosive story. She wanted to discuss this information with someone who would value her work and tenacity, at the same time hoping to gain the fame and status she so desperately yearned for in the journalistic sphere in Egypt. The information she had was so incriminating to the people involved that she feared for her own life.

"Mona, you look so scared and mentally drained, dear," her husband of 12 years said. "Are you sure you want to go forward with this? You haven't had a decent night's sleep in weeks," he continued with genuine, heartfelt concern.

"I've worked so hard to uncover the web of deception in this story. It's a matter of national security, and I was never one to shy away from my duty as an investigative journalist," she said. Her hand was shaking as she folded the lined piece of paper and put it in her red shoulder bag.

Mona left the bedroom and headed directly to the kitchen to make herself a warm mug of coffee before going out for her daily morning walk. She spread her favorite hummus paste onto a slice of bread and washed it down with some cool water before changing into her sweat pants and oversized sweatshirt. Despite the chilly weather this morning, she was determined to get some fresh air to calm her anxiety.

Mona walked around her area in *Zamalek* almost every morning, except on weekends when she preferred to relax at home with her husband and son. Today, she felt completely drained, both mentally and physically, but she still walked the same route, greeting the newspaper man at the end of her street with a smile. She wanted to pretend everything was normal, when in fact all she felt was palpable fear. She was deep in thought as she walked by the flower shop, the grocery store, and the café, wondering whether she should go to the proposed meeting at the Imperial Hotel. She didn't like the idea of handing over sensitive material in a hotel setting, much preferring to meet somewhere outdoors where she could have her husband watch over her from afar.

Her husband was steadfast against the idea of her turning in such dangerous material at a hotel, but given the sensitivity of the material, he eventually acquiesced. Mona had stored all the evidence on a flash drive and printed out a hard copy, which she hid in her husband's safe, just in case the flash drive got damaged or stolen. She never wrote down the names of the five people implicated in her story except on a lined piece of paper, which she kept in her red bag. She didn't want the names on the list to be exposed by anyone other than herself.

By eight o'clock that night, Mona became extremely tense as she got dressed in a pair of black pants and a red faux fur cardigan. She was repeatedly reassured that this was the safest means for her to hand over the information she had to trusted parties. It was also deemed too dangerous for her to be seen speaking to someone in public due to the presence of closed-circuit cameras in the hotel lobby and hallways.

Mona didn't have the nerves to drive tonight. She ordered an Uber to the Imperial hotel, since parking around the hotel was infamous for being overly congested anyway. She entered the hotel at exactly 10 minutes before nine and headed directly to the Maharaja restaurant as instructed. The maître D' greeted her with a welcoming smile at the entrance and showed her to her table. He handed her the menu and jotted down her order three minutes later, but Mona didn't have any appetite tonight. Her stomach and thoughts were both in shambles. She hurriedly finished her meal and opened her wallet to take out some cash and the flash drive. She waved to the maître D' and discreetly handed him the flash drive wrapped inside some paper bills. He reached out and took them with his white gloved hand, after which he instructed her to go directly to Suite 55 on the fifth floor, where she would have the privacy to speak at length about the information she had gathered. He then nonchalantly disappeared through a side door.

Mona was extremely nervous about this unexpected change of plan, feeling extremely anxious about meeting total strangers in a hotel room. She sat in her seat, analyzing the options before her. She could either walk away from the hotel now or she could go to Suite 55 and have the privacy she needed to explain her story. After all, she had already just handed in her flash drive. Her journalistic conscience kept nagging her to fulfill her professional and moral duty, whereas her ego kept begging for fame and recognition. She eventually succumbed, exited the restaurant, and reluctantly searched for the nearest elevator. Her hands shook as she pressed the elevator button up to the fifth floor.

The elevator door opened to a posh carpeted entrance with long hallways on both ends, adorned with gold rimmed mirrors and mahogany paneled walls. Mona caught her breath as she looked at the gold-plated black arrow, which pointed her in the direction of Suite 55. She looked at her reflection in the mirror on the right hand side and stopped briefly to make sure she looked presentable. Her knees began to tremble as she approached her designated suite.

Once she spotted the shiny mahogany doors of Suite 55, Mona stopped, breathed in deeply, and adjusted her clothes. She clutched her red bag tightly and knocked firmly three times on the door. She couldn't hear any movement or footsteps inside. Then the door opened slowly. She couldn't see who was standing there because of the dim lighting.

She steadied herself and walked inside…

Chapter Two
'Body of Evidence'

It was a cloudy, chilly Monday morning. Camillia knew she had to be at work on time despite hearing her mother's loud coughs from across the dimly lit, very narrow hallway. Her mother had been sick since the winter crept its way in by early December. This year, winter had started early and was unusually cold and frosty in Cairo.

Their dilapidated two-bedroom flat in *Boulaq El-Dakrour* district was in dire need of new glass windows, and the paint was peeling off the ceiling in sloughs, courtesy of the neighbors upstairs who repeatedly refused to hire a plumber to stop the leakage.

"I'm going to have to go to work, *Hajja*," Camillia called out to her mother, who was slipping in and out of sleep due to the excessive cough medicine she'd been taking for the past three days.

Camillia feared her mother's lungs wouldn't be able to handle the onslaught of a second bout of pneumonia. Camillia referred to her mother as *Hajja* as a show of respect, even though her mother, Nadia, had never gone on pilgrimage before. Camillia's brother, Mohsen, worked in Saudi Arabia as a construction worker, sending them as much money as he could spare every month, which was barely enough to cover their food and rent, leaving Camillia with no choice but to work at the housekeeping department of the prestigious Imperial Hotel, in the affluent neighborhood of *Zamalek* in Cairo.

Cleaning was all Camillia knew how to do for a living, having left school after the sixth grade to help take care of her mother's expenses as well as her own ambitions to make something out of her life. Her father had passed away at the age of 42 after suffering a sudden stroke. He was a heavy smoker who relished sitting with his group of rogue friends at the *qahwa* at the end of the road, smoking a water pipe, making dirty jokes, and playing backgammon almost every night till past midnight.

Camillia was always the first to arrive at the housekeeping department every morning at seven o'clock sharp, working hard till eight at night, except for Tuesdays, when she worked a half-day shift till two o'clock in the afternoon. Her mother had also worked as a cleaner, but that was before her fragile lungs had suffered from cystic fibrosis, after which she decided to settle for a less hectic job. She now worked from home, crocheting jumpers and table runners for meager prices. Camillia had learned all the tricks of her cleaning trade by watching her mother clean their own small, stuffy flat, both women attempting to make the best of what they had and thanking *Allah* that they had a roof over their heads, even if that roof was literally falling apart.

Nadia constantly nagged Camillia to try to find a comfortably wealthy man, but at her current age of 30, no well-to-do suitors had asked for her hand in marriage. Much to Nadia's dismay, as she had hoped her attractive daughter would settle down and have kids before she became too old for motherhood. Camillia, on the other hand, was always nonchalant about the subject of marriage but was nonetheless thankful that she was endowed with a naturally slim figure, large brown eyes, and soft, silky black hair.

Marriage was not what Camillia aspired to. She had two cousins who were already divorced by the age of 25, both single mothers suffering to make ends meet. Camillia wanted a better life for herself, trying to save as much money as she could in order to travel to a Gulf country, much like her brother had done. She wanted to make a better living and live independently rather than live in servitude to a man who would usurp her freedom, most likely divorcing her and leaving her with two or three children to rear on her own.

Camillia patiently sat inside the usual white microbus, feeling uncomfortable as the bearded man beside her kept reaching into his pocket and leaning toward her as if by accident. She had gotten used to the harassment on her commutes to and from work, as she immediately adjusted her headscarf, as if by doing so she would somehow make herself invisible to the men around her. The driver kept honking his horn every few meters until finally, much to Camillia's relief, he reached the stop where she disembarked every morning at seven o'clock.

She walked hurriedly toward the narrow back street of the Imperial Hotel, as she had done every morning for the past five years. The cold wind was pushing against her back, giving her added speed as she made her way toward the 'staff only' entrance, where she pulled out her name tag and flashed it at the security guard.

"Good morning, Saber, how are you today?" Camillia asked, not really caring to hear his response.

She was well acquainted with all four security guards who took shifts at that staff entrance, and they all knew better than to mess with Camillia. She was known for being a hard-working, no nonsense woman who would answer back quite aggressively if anyone attempted to cross the line with her. She walked into the housekeeping department and headed directly toward her locker, where she quickly changed into her uniform to commence her shift on the fifth floor.

Camillia knew the fifth floor of the Imperial Hotel as if it were her own home. She had to make sure that all five suites on this floor were immaculately cleaned, restocked with toilet paper, towels, clean sheets, toothpaste, shampoo, soap, and mini boxes of Godiva milk chocolate. She would often wish she could slip a toiletry kit into the housecleaning supply trolley, which she routinely pushed down the hall every morning, but she would always decide against it. She wanted to maintain her stellar reputation of honesty amongst hotel staff and managers, knowing that *Allah* would reward her for her patience.

Camillia pushed her house cleaning trolley down the hallway, making sure the suite tags were turned toward the green 'clean room please' sign before making her way inside using her black magnetic card. She knew exactly what to do, confidently entering each suite, cleaning and restocking supplies. She finally made her way to Suite 55, which was the largest and most prestigious at the Imperial hotel. Camillia stopped her supply trolley in front of the shiny mahogany wooden door, making sure the green sign was hanging from the round stainless steel door knob. She was so accustomed to being met by the sight of mangled white sheets and purple bed covers, as well as the usual clothing items sprawled across the king size bed. She always expected to see toothpaste residue in the double vanity sinks as well as dirty Limoges plates and silver-plated cutlery on the oval coffee table, which was purposely positioned in front of the huge glass window which overlooked the murky green Nile below.

Upon entering the suite, Camillia could smell a very familiar stench. She was certain it was the faint odor of bleach or a strong cleaning detergent. She cautiously walked inside the suite, carefully minding her steps as the heavy curtains had been tightly drawn together, plunging the suite into near complete darkness. She made her way all the way to the window and pulled one of the curtains open, then made her way to the other side, pulling the other curtain back as well.

Camillia turned around to face the king-size bed, expecting to see the usual unkempt bed sheets and clothing items, only to be startled to find the bedding completely gone. The king-size bed lay bare, stripped of all its soft white cotton sheets and pillows. She had never encountered missing sheets and pillows before in any of the five suites on the fifth floor during her five-year tenure at the hotel. She wondered how this could have happened, given that she had checked the suite the evening before and everything was in its usual place.

She could sense a brewing knot in her stomach, as something seemed to be off in Suite 55 this morning. Camillia walked to the bathroom, expecting to find half-empty miniature bottles of shampoo laying on the countertop and dirty towels thrown carelessly under the double vanity sinks, but much to her surprise, there were no used towels or toiletries anywhere. The bathroom was completely barren, as if no guests had ever used it before. Camillia started to feel a rush of adrenaline surge inside her, which in turn amplified her five senses, as if she were about to encounter a pouncing enemy. She exited the barren bathroom, walking back to the mahogany oval coffee table in front of the large glass window, feeling a sense of determination to find any trace of the previous guests. Camillia was never faced by this odd situation before.

The knot in her stomach tugged even more as she began to worry that her manager, Mr. Hamed, might reprimand her for all the missing items, which, in her mind, had been deliberately taken from the suite. She walked to the naked king-size bed and noticed that even the hotel's elegant black pen and leather case notepad had been removed from the bed-side table on the left side of the bed. She stopped still when her eyes caught a glimpse of three oblong, brownish-red dots on the bright yellow wallpaper above the bed-side table. She could feel a sheen of sweat wash over her body as she realized that those three stains could either be dirt or neglected evidence of some sort of injury or foul play. Sheer fear now gripped her as she began to meticulously search the suite for any other oddities.

Her trained eyes traveled all across the yellowish-red lotus patterned carpeting, scanning for stains and dirt. She wanted to find anything on the lavish carpeting that could either make her rush to hotel security or simply report the missing items to her manager. She returned to the mahogany suite door and slowly began walking down the short hallway, all the way to the glass window. She couldn't find any telltale signs of anything unusual until she reached the oval mahogany table, which was flanked by two upholstered armchairs on either side. The chair to the right of the table had a slightly visible, long brownish-red stain on the seat itself. The carpet beneath that chair had a visible, round, discolored stain. Camillia bent down to touch the carpet stain and found it rough to the touch, as if it had been recently scrubbed. She also caught the same faint odor of bleach which she had whiffed as she entered the suite.

Camillia wasn't sure whether the three stains on the wallpaper, the stain on the chair, and the discolored patch of carpet under the chair had been there for a considerable time or whether they were left behind by yesterday's odd guests, who had decided to wipe out all the items in the suite before they checked out late last night. She was just about to leave the suite when she saw a piece of paper trapped underneath the heavy curtain to the right of the glass window. She picked it up and found that it was a notepad size sheet of lined paper, folded in half, bent in a few places here and there, but the writing in blue ink was nonetheless clearly visible.

The paper had a list of names numbered from one to five. Camillia immediately recognized two of the names: that of Farida El Leithy, a media figure, and Marwan El Meligy, a well-known shipping magnate, albeit with a somewhat shady reputation. The other three names were unfamiliar to her. She folded the piece of paper and slipped it in her undershirt rather than in her pocket, wanting to make sure it didn't get lost before she handed it to the 'lost and found' department. She exited the room and decided to go to her manager to report the missing items as well as the three suspicious stains on the wallpaper, the stain on the chair, and the discolored stain on the carpet. She was just about to enter the housecleaning department located on the first floor when she saw two of her female colleagues walk hurriedly out of the glass doors in a state of sheer panic. She then saw her manager follow suit with a look of utter fear on his face.

"What's happening, Mr. Hamed? Did something happen?" she loudly reiterated, the knot in her stomach seemingly devouring her entire being.

"There's been a murder! They just found a female body outside the hotel in a dumpster!" he yelled, running to the staff elevator at the end of the hallway.

Chapter Three
'The Police Officer'

Camillia's face was drained of all color as it immediately dawned on her that the oddities she had just witnessed in Suite 55 could well be connected to this murder. She hurried to her locker to grab her cellphone in an effort to snap some shots from the suite, which she thought could potentially be used as evidence in case there really had been foul play. She ran out of breath as she dashed back to Suite 55, almost knocking over an elderly female tourist who was slowly walking down the corridor. Camillia entered the suite once again using her card key, hurriedly snapped shots of the three stains on the wallpaper, the long stain on the chair, the white discolored stain on the carpet, the barren bathroom, and the stark naked bed. She switched her phone to silent mode and carefully hid it in her undershirt next to the piece of lined paper.

Camillia then rushed to the hotel's main lobby, where a number of her colleagues and hotel guests were gathered, all of them speaking at once in a rising crescendo. They were all staring outside the double-height glass windows, where two policemen were speaking to the hotel manager and two of the front desk clerks. "What's happening, Hend?" Camillia asked her colleague, who looked panic-stricken amidst all the commotion.

"The security guards in the back street reported finding a dead woman's body in one of the dumpsters," Hend responded in a hurry, looking scared and flushed.

"Was she a guest here in the hotel?" Camillia pressed on, trying to gather as much information as possible. She knew the discovery of a murdered guest would irreparably damage the reputation of the hotel.

"I don't know! It's all happening right now as we speak!" Hend answered, leaving Camillia and melting into the swelling crowd in the lobby. Camillia spotted her manager, Mr. Hamed, and rushed toward him, bumping into a group of tourists who were speaking a foreign language which she didn't understand.

"Mr. Hamed, was the female victim a guest here at the hotel?" Camillia asked, her anxiety reaching unprecedented heights when she saw the alarmed look on his face.

"We don't know anything for now except that the female body was found in the street behind the hotel, in one of the dumpsters!" he said in a loud voice. "The security guards found the body 20 minutes ago and are being questioned by police right now."

"Mr. Hamed, there's something I need to report to you," Camillia said, raising her voice a notch so her manager could hear her. "I don't know if this strange incident is related to the crime being investigated," she said, resting her hand on her chest, making sure the piece of paper and her phone were still in place in her undershirt.

Her manager motioned for her to follow him to a nearby corridor near the emergency exit, where they could speak privately away from all the noise.

"What is it?" Mr. Hamed asked, his thick mustache glistening under the neon light. He was clearly feeling impatient and eager to go back to the lobby to watch the scene unfold. He kept tugging at his shirt cuffs, looking extremely nervous and uneasy.

"I was cleaning Suite 55 as I do every day, but this morning I found some strange reddish-brown smears on the wallpaper as well as a brownish-red streak on one of the armchairs and a large white stain on the carpet under the same chair," Camillia said as fast as she could muster.

"It could just be dirt left behind by guests; *Allah* knows we see that all the time," he said, as he began to walk away toward the lobby.

"Mr. Hamed, wait! The bed was also stripped of all its sheets and pillows, and all the towels were missing too!" Camillia said, trailing close behind him.

He stopped and turned around to face her.

"Has that ever happened before since you began working here?" he asked, obviously beginning to take keen interest in what she was saying to him.

"No! I have never seen a hotel suite stripped of all items this way on the fifth floor!" she said, sensing the knot in her stomach returning with a vengeance. "Suite 55 is known to be one of the most prestigious suites in this hotel. Why would guests take sheets, pillows, and towels with them?" she asked.

Mr. Hamed nodded his head in agreement, his graying hairline showing beads of sweat. He told her that he would report this incident to hotel security. Feeling satisfied that she had said what she had to say, Camillia followed her boss back to the lobby, where the crowd was even larger than it had been a few minutes earlier.

Maged El Miniawy, the police officer in charge on the scene, had solved three murder cases in the affluent *Zamalek* area of Cairo and had been asked to head a task force to investigate this murder. His boss had called him into his office an hour ago to brief him that a female body had been discovered in a dumpster outside the posh Imperial Hotel. Maged immediately sped toward the site, accompanied by two other officers. He knew from past experience that he would be under immense pressure to gather information quickly, carefully, and methodically, having to comb the crime scene from top to bottom with his forensic team.

He had arrived on the back street of the hotel within minutes and immediately spotted three hotel security guards gathered around a particular dark green dumpster. He ran toward them and asked if they recalled seeing anything suspicious in the street during the past few hours. They all reported seeing nothing unusual until 20 minutes prior, when the garbage truck arrived to pick up the black plastic bags from the large dumpsters, which belonged exclusively to the hotel. They described how the garbage collector had yelled out for the security guards on duty when he smelled a foul stench emanating from the dumpster in question. The three security guards had run toward the dumpster and tore open the garbage bag to find the body of a fully dressed woman with a clear bloodied injury to the front of her head.

"What time does the garbage truck come for pick-up every day?" Maged asked the security guards, trying to ascertain an immediate timeline for when the body could have been placed there.

"It arrives around seven o' clock every morning," Saber responded, as he unbuttoned his collar in a clear sign of distress.

"So, the body must have been placed in the dumpster anywhere between seven in the morning yesterday and seven o'clock in the morning today," Maged said to his colleague, who had already placed a yellow police tape three meters around the dumpster.

The other two officers had quickly lined both ends of the back street with bright red cones, barring vehicles and pedestrians from contaminating the crime scene. Maged quickly walked around to the main entrance of the hotel, where he was met by the hotel manager, who was already pacing the sidewalk in a state of panic. Maged identified himself as the officer in charge and ordered that all personnel on duty at the hotel gather together in the lobby for interrogation.

Camillia watched the scene unfold from inside the lobby, observing the hotel manager as he quickly entered the hotel, accompanied by a dark-haired, muscular police officer who had a visible mole under one eye. Both men headed directly to Mr. Hamed, exchanged a few words with him before dispersing hurriedly in different directions. She then noticed how Mr. Hamed was nervously watching the crowd in the lobby until his eyes wandered toward her. He rushed in her direction, elbowing his way through the thickening crowd.

"Camillia, you and all housekeeping personnel have to be questioned by police right now! You have to report what you saw in Suite 55 even though the police still don't know if this victim was a guest here or if she was even connected to this hotel in any way," he said, sweat dripping profusely on his creased white shirt.

"Of course, of course! Who should I talk to?" Camillia asked as she looked around anxiously for the muscular police officer.

"Officer Maged El Miniawy is the police officer in charge! Come with me! I think I see him over there speaking to the front desk clerks!" Hamed shouted.

Camillia's legs felt weak. She began to shudder once they approached the officer. She had never been questioned by a police officer before, and she felt very nervous as he turned sideways to look at them.

"Maged *basha*, this is Camillia, one of my house cleaning staff. There was an incident that happened this morning in one of the suites on the fifth floor," Mr. Hamed said, giving Camillia the cue to begin speaking, before walking away.

"Mr. Maged, I don't know if this incident has anything to do with the body found outside, but I'll tell you everything anyway, if you think it's important!" she said, her face now red and flustered.

"Go ahead Camillia. Tell me what happened this morning," Maged said, feeling a sight rush of adrenaline begin to kick in.

"I arrived at work at seven o'clock sharp and headed to the fifth floor, which is the most prestigious here at the hotel, to restock and clean the suites as I do every morning. Once I arrived at Suite 55, I noticed a number of odd things!" she said, as she watched his face closely for signs of intrigue.

"Odd things? Like what? Camillia, please focus and remember clearly," he said, grabbing a notepad and pen from the front desk.

Once she saw the seriousness in his eyes, she continued on with more confidence. "The suite had an odor of bleach or cleaning substance, and there were three reddish-brown dots on the wallpaper, a stain under one of the chairs, and a long reddish-brown streak on the same chair!" she said quickly, eyeing the officer as he jotted down his notes.

"This may be relevant to the case, but is there anything else you noticed in any of the suites you cleaned during the past 24 hours?" he asked, his eyes locking in with hers.

"Yes! The bedding and towels were completely removed from Suite 55," she added, noticing his hazel eye color.

Maged raised an eyebrow as he made another entry on the notepad. "Thank you, Camillia. Is there anything else you want to say?" Maged asked as his eyes drifted across the lobby as if searching for other staff members to question.

"No! That's all I have to say," Camillia said with a slight hesitation as she felt the piece of lined paper rub against her skin.

Maged made a final note with his pen and turned away in a hurry. He had many other people to question, and time was of the essence, but he made a mental note to question Camillia at length once again at the police station. Camillia walked away from Maged and was about to head to the housekeeping department when Mr. Hamed called out to her.

"You cannot leave the hotel until the police are done with questioning all personnel!" he yelled.

"But I already spoke to the officer and told him everything," Camillia said, feeling the warmth of her phone in her undershirt.

Mr. Hamed ignored her remark and walked away, his white shirt even more drenched with sweat now. Camillia decided to discreetly linger in the lobby, choosing a tall artificial palm tree for cover. She observed how the police officers were taking a few front desk clerks aside for questioning and how the hotel guests were nervously whispering amongst themselves. She wanted to call her mother to tell her what had happened and that she may be back home later than usual.

Chapter Four
'The Widower'

Maged had four more housekeeping staff members to talk to before he finally gave them all permission to go home. It was five o'clock in the afternoon, and all the staff members were already looking drained. Maged and his assistants did their best to grill them for information, while forensic team investigators were busy identifying the female victim in a rush to run her photo through the national police data system.

It wasn't long before the victim was identified as Mona El Safty, a 43 year old freelance investigative reporter with a reputation for exposing high stakes social and political news stories. Her husband had reported her missing to the police in *Zamalek* the night before she failed to return home. Maged wanted to interview him as soon as possible to find out if Mona was meeting someone at the hotel or whether she had been there at all. Given the sketchy information Maged had collected so far from hotel personnel, he desperately needed details and in-depth information from her husband. He was also being pressured by his superiors at the police department to solve this murder as soon as possible.

Not wanting to wait any longer to question the victim's husband, Maged decided to leave the hotel and head directly to Mona's apartment. Her husband showed him inside to the living room, where Maged noticed how clean and orderly the place was.

"I'm so sorry for your loss, Mr. Karim," Maged said, his voice sounding deeper than usual. "I assure you we will do everything we possibly can to bring those responsible to justice," he said, his eyes focused on the man in front of him.

"I told her not to go to the Imperial Hotel! I told her this investigative story was too dangerous and that she was putting her life at risk!" he sobbed as his tears fell onto his white shirt. He clasped his hands together tightly, rubbing the sweat off the back of his neck.

"Why did she go to the hotel?" Maged asked. "Was she meeting someone there?" he continued. Maged knew that he needed to rule out, beyond a shadow of a doubt, that the victim's husband could be her killer. In the previous case he had solved, the 28 year old wife was strangled by her husband for going out of the house several times without asking his permission.

"She told me she was about to expose an explosive story, one which involved high-profile names," he sobbed. "She went to great lengths and danger to put the pieces together," he said, his eyes bloodshot from lack of sleep.

"What was this story about, and who did it involve?" Maged asked, his adrenaline spiking.

"She didn't want to tell me the names for my own safety, but she did tell me that it was about dangerous liaisons between people in power here and some powerful entity abroad," he said, burying his head in his hands.

"Did she show you any papers or any evidence of this?" Maged asked, hoping to get his hands on any material which would corroborate the husband's story.

"Yes, she hid something in the safe in our bedroom," he said, pointing to the room off the hallway. "I'll go get it!" he said, as he walked away with a slight limp.

Maged took this time alone in the living room to look at the framed family photos on the walls, in an attempt to try to get a feel for the energy in the place. He wondered if Mona's husband was telling the truth or whether they were a couple embroiled in domestic violence and infidelity.

"Here! Here! I found these papers in my safe!" the widower shouted, his face showing signs of emotional pain mingled with relief.

Maged took the file and skimmed through it, finding handwritten notes on small lined paper as well as typed documents. He told Karim that he would admit this file as important case evidence and that he needed to know any information possible about Mona's explosive journalistic story.

"Who was she going to meet at the hotel?" Maged asked, hoping to get a name or two that would put a quick end to this case.

"She wasn't going to meet anybody," the widower said, his voice becoming lower as if in shame.

"What do you mean? What was she doing there then?" Maged pressed on, his optimism taking a sudden nosedive.

"She was told to go to the Indian restaurant at the Imperial Hotel to turn in the information she had stored on her flash drive to the maître d'. That was all. It was supposed to be risk-free and safe," he said, his face twisting with agony.

"The maître d'? That's very strange. Why wasn't she going to hand in her information to someone else in person?" Maged asked, thinking out loud to himself.

"She was told that this was the safest way for her to turn in her information. They refused to hold any face-to-face meetings," the widower answered, his face growing crimson with anger. "You have to catch those bastards! You have to bring us justice!" he shouted, his neck veins bulging out.

"Who told her to go to this meeting at the hotel?" Maged asked calmly, trying to get a name or any cue to help him move forward in an increasingly interesting and peculiar case.

"I don't know! She would get these instructional messages from time to time on her phone. I don't know who she was speaking to about her story or if anyone else helped her dig up this information," he said, his voice growing weary.

Maged decided to leave the conversation there and return to the police station to examine the file in his hand. He told Karim to stay seated and that he would show himself out.

Before leaving the apartment, Maged remembered to ask something.

"Mr. Karim, where's your son?" he asked.

"I sent him to my mother's house. I couldn't bear the pain of breaking the news to him about his mother today," the widower answered, as a couple of tears rolled down his face.

Chapter Five
'The Interrogation'

Mr. Hamed gave Camillia permission to go home but told her that Officer Maged wanted to question her at the police station early the next morning. She felt physically drained and weary as she opened the door to her small apartment, feeling the heat of her phone and the folded piece of paper rub against her skin. Her chest felt sore from the friction.

Her mother was sitting at the small kitchen table stuffing a few green peppers with rice, looking better today than she had during the past few days. Camillia greeted her in a somber tone, feeling tired but at the same time desperately wanting to tell her about the murder.

"What's wrong, Camillia?" Nadia immediately asked, peering at her with concern. "Is something bothering you today dear?"

"Yes, *Hajja*. They found a body in a dumpster outside the hotel this morning!" Camillia said as the paper pinched her chest, as if begging for release.

"Oh no! A body! What happened?" Nadia gasped, clutching her nightdress with her rough hands and dropping the hollow green pepper onto the wooden table.

"The police aren't sure whether the female victim was killed in the hotel or not, but I think she was. There were strange things in Suite 55 this morning. I told Mr. Hamed about the odd things I saw, and he said he would report it to hotel security. I was then questioned by a police officer, and I told him everything. But I still have to go to the police station tomorrow morning for further questioning," Camillia said, looking uneasy and feeling scared.

Her mother looked at her with deep concern, feeling distressed that her only daughter was going to a police station to be questioned in a murder case. Trusting her daughter's street smart ways, Nadia immediately brushed her fears aside, and put her daughter's fate in *Allah's* hands.

Camillia walked to her small bedroom and immediately removed her phone and the lined piece of paper from her undershirt. The paper was crumpled up and dampened with sweat, but the names were still visible. She smoothed out the crumpled parts with her hands and placed the paper in her closet under a pile of clothes, so that it would be flat by morning. She planned on turning in the list to the 'lost and found' department after she finished her meeting with Officer Maged. She then switched her phone to regular mode and immediately heard a beep. It was a new text message.

It was from an unknown number. She read the text message out loud:

"I know you have the paper. Don't show it to anyone. If you do, *your body will be next in a trash bag.*"

Camillia's hands trembled, and her heart began to beat very rapidly. She felt so scared that her body began to shudder, and she began to pace around frantically in her small bedroom. She didn't want her mother to know anything about the piece of paper, lest her life be endangered too. She was now certain that whomever had sent this message knew that she was the one who had cleaned Suite 55. It also confirmed her earlier suspicions that Suite 55 may have been the scene of possible foul play. She was doubly terrified that the perpetrator knew her phone number, and she immediately decided to change it, only to realize that her phone could be the only liaison to catch the killer.

Camillia was now in a mental warp, as she now feared the grave consequences of testifying to Officer Maged about the threatening text message. She believed that the only way for her to safely navigate this quagmire was for her to go to the police station and reiterate her testimony to the officer, but to refrain from mentioning anything about the piece of paper or the death threat.

She tossed and turned all night, trying to figure out how the killer had found out that she was the housekeeper who had last cleaned Suite 55, given that the housekeeping roster was only privy to Mr. Hamed and her colleagues. Her heart began to race wildly at the sheer prospect that Mr. Hamed or somebody in her department could be in direct contact with the killer or even be the killer himself. Having had no sleep whatsoever, Camillia was both mentally and emotionally exhausted. She concluded that if Mr. Hamed was an accomplice or accessory to this murder, then it would surely mean that her job was at risk. She now felt that she must comply with the killer's wishes and that she was now facing the imminent loss of her one and only source of income.

By seven o'clock in the morning, Camillia was already dressed in her long brown skirt and long white top, donning a matching brown headscarf. She avoided any eye contact with her mother and opted to skip breakfast under the pretense that she may be late to the interrogation. She didn't want her ailing mother to suffer the same agonizing terror that she was going through herself.

She decided to go to the police station as early as possible and to head to the hotel thereafter. Her heart was beating wildly as she stepped out of the minibus, making her way to the entrance of the police station. She asked for Officer Maged and was directed to a room at the end of a narrow corridor. Her knees trembled. The door was open, and Camillia could see Maged sitting at a desk, impatiently looking through some papers. There was another officer sitting across the desk from him. She coughed to signal her presence, and Maged immediately looked up at her, gesturing for her to take a seat.

"Camillia, I'm glad you're here early. I need you to tell me everything you saw in Suite 55 again. We are analyzing all the hotel's surveillance cameras as we speak, so it's only a matter of time and we'll catch this murderer," he said, eyeing her carefully.

The other officer clicked his pen and got ready to write down her testimony.

"Well, as I told you yesterday, I don't know if this is connected to the murder, but I noticed some odd things in Suite 55," Camillia said, her heart beating very rapidly now.

"Tell me again exactly what you saw," Maged asked, as he pressed the record button on his recording device.

"I entered the suite and found the bedding and towels completely gone, and there were three reddish-brown dots on the wallpaper next to the bed," Camillia said, trying to catch her breath and calm her fear. "There was also a stain on one armchair and a stain on the carpet underneath the armchair. I also smelled wisps of cleaning detergent when I entered the suite," she said, feeling completely out of breath at this point.

"Did you notice anything else, Camillia? Were there any items left behind by the guests?" Maged asked, his gut instincts telling him to probe deeper.

"Items? Items like what?" Camillia asked, her heart beating out of control. She self-consciously adjusted her headscarf and pursed her lips together.

"I ask the questions here!" Maged said, sensing her anxiety and nervousness. "Are you the only housekeeper who cleans this suite, or is there somebody else who cleans this suite on another shift?" Maged asked.

"I'm the only housekeeper who covers the 12 hour shift between seven in the morning and seven in the evening," Camillia said, feeling increasingly uneasy. "When I'm absent from work, only then does a colleague cover my 12 hour shift."

"I sent a forensic team to collect evidence from Suite 55, immediately following the testimony you gave me yesterday, Camillia. It's peculiar that they didn't find evidence of dots on the wallpaper, or any other stains around the armchairs," Maged said. "How do you explain that?" he asked slowly, his eyes watching her intently.

"I told you exactly what I saw yesterday morning in the suite. I also told Mr. Hamed and he said he would report it to hotel security," Camillia said, as she began to sweat profusely, despite the cold weather outside.

"Cameras in the hallway show that you returned to Suite 55, approximately 10 minutes after you first cleaned it. Why did you return to the suite, Camillia?" Maged asked, trusting his hunch that there was something she was hiding from him.

"I returned to take photos on my phone of the oddities I saw after Mr. Hamed told me that a body had been found outside the hotel in a dumpster," Camillia replied, feeling the noose tighten around her neck.

"So you have photos on your phone of the oddities in Suite 55, and yet you didn't mention that to me?" Maged asked, ascertaining that the woman in front of him wasn't being forthcoming in her testimony.

"I wasn't sure yesterday when I took the photos that it was related to the murder. If the detectives found no evidence in the suite, then I have the evidence. I'm not a liar," Camillia said, looking at the officer with defiance.

Camillia handed her phone to the officer, knowing that he was going to ask to see the photos. She had already deleted the threatening text message out of fear of being implicated in the murder if her phone fell into the wrong hands.

Maged took the phone and examined the photos carefully. He then gave her back the phone and told her she was dismissed but that she should call him if she remembered any other details. Camillia got up to leave and was about to exit the interrogation room when Maged asked her a question that made her freeze in her tracks.

"Camillia, you seem sure today that Suite 55 is connected to the murder. I never told you it was," he said, as he rolled his pen around his pointer and forefinger.

"Sorry, I just assumed so. I'm just trying to help the police," Camillia answered back, faking a smile.

"I'm sure you'll be of great help to us," Maged replied, faking a smile of his own.

Chapter Six
'The Mole, the Magnate, and the Mogul'

Assem had just finished his shift at the *Zamalek* police station and headed directly to the coffee shop in the crowded and bustling *Khan El Khalili* area, where they had agreed to meet.

"How could this happen?" Marwan whispered to the man sitting across the small rectangular table from him as he adjusted his dark sunglasses.

"I could be asking you the same question!" Assem answered back as he tried to control his anger. "All I know is that this woman knows our names," he said as quietly as he could, looking around him for fear of being followed. "I will find a way to silence her. She needs money and can't afford to lose her job. Leave the woman to me," Assem whispered with confidence.

Marwan got up to leave, not wanting to linger in public much longer. But before leaving, he placed a small white plastic bag on the small table between them. Assem put the bag in the inside pocket of his jacket and finished sipping his hot Turkish coffee before hopping onto a dented white microbus that was parked around the corner. Being the seasoned police officer that he was, Assem knew his life was now on the line and that he couldn't afford to let Camillia out of his sight. He also knew that his life meant absolutely nothing to the people he was working for. He was simply their mole to the insider police information which they desperately needed. But Assem knew how to use this connection to cash in handsome amounts of money.

He got off the microbus and headed directly to the hotel, where he knew she would be, having already examined the housekeeping roster on the day of the murder. The fact that he was one of two police officers who were on the scene of the crime with Maged, had guaranteed him unrestricted access to sensitive information. That was how he had found out that Camillia was the last staff member to visit Suite 55. He had already changed into civilian clothing before leaving the police station, in an effort to blend in with the public, when he met Marwan at the coffee shop. Being out of uniform was also the most convenient way for him to watch Camillia without attracting attention. He needed to approach her without coming across as intimidating. If anything, Assem needed her to consider him the 'good cop.'

Having already studied the floor plan of the Imperial hotel, he went directly to the housekeeping department located on the first floor. He needed to neutralize Camillia's threat to the operation, and he already knew what buttons he needed to push in order to make her cave in. He was here to execute a plan which would ensure that she would never think of revealing the names on the list to Maged or to anyone else.

Mr. Hamed was in the midst of a staff meeting when Assem walked through the doorway. Both men nodded at one another, as they had already met in the lobby during staff interrogation the previous morning. Assem wasn't sure what Camillia looked like, so he asked Mr. Hamed to point her out.

"Camillia, I hope you're trying hard to remember everything you can about the suite," Assem said, as he approached her, looking her straight in the eye.

"Who are you? I already told Officer Maged this morning everything I saw in the suite," she answered, with some defiance.

"I know you were at the station this morning. I'm Officer Assem, Maged's assistant on the case. You are a very important witness for us," Assem said, trying to inflate her ego.

"Officer Maged already told me to contact him if I needed to," she said, looking away rather impatiently.

"You can always contact me as well. Officer Maged and I are on the same team. Here's my number if you remember anything new. Every moment counts, Camillia," Assem said with a friendly grin.

Camillia slipped the card reluctantly into her pocket, reassuring the officer that she would do everything possible to assist the police. Assem wondered if that was the same pocket she had used to hide the list of names as he watched her slim figure walk away. He lingered around the hallway for a few minutes before going to the housekeeping locker room. He searched for Camillia's name tag and spotted her locker in the middle row. After making sure there were no cameras or staff members anywhere in sight, he slipped on a pair of latex gloves and carefully opened Camillia's locker, where he found her shoulder bag. He took the small white plastic bag, which Marwan had given him, out of his pocket and carefully wiped it before placing it in Camillia's zipper compartment.

Assem then headed out of the housekeeping department, down to the lobby, and out of the Imperial hotel. He had no time to waste playing games with Camillia. He calculated his moves very well and simply cut to the chase. That's why he was considered to be a stellar policeman, getting assigned to very complex murder cases during the past two years. He absolutely meant what he wrote when he sent Camillia the text message earlier this morning. Now he hoped she would get the message loud and clear.

A few kilometers away, Marwan had parked his black Jeep outside his trendy downtown office. He had always feared being seen in public with Assem, and he rarely ventured too far away from the bustling downtown area of Cairo. But today, he was compelled to meet Assem in person in order to emphasize the gravity of the situation. He was under pressure to reassure his superiors that he had the situation under control and that he had great confidence in Assem's highly persuasive ways. Having repeatedly dealt with the greedy, arrogant police officer, Marwan knew that Assem would do whatever was needed to ensure the success of this operation.

Marwan also knew that the people he was dealing with were not ones to cross and that they had powerful loyalists everywhere. He was well aware that he could easily be replaced with another shipping operator if Assem failed to control Camillia. Marwan couldn't afford to lose his lucrative connection with these people, owing much of the success of his shipping business to their generous financial patronage.

As soon as he walked into his office, his secretary rushed to tell him that a woman had been waiting for him in the reception. Marwan calmly sat at his desk, then told his secretary to allow the visitor to come in.

"Marwan El Meligy!" the woman said, as she entered the room and took a seat across the desk from him, with a flamboyant flair.

"Yes, how can I help you?" Marwan asked, eyeing the attractive woman with interest. He thought that she looked familiar, but he couldn't quite remember where he had seen her.

"You don't know me?" the woman asked in a low voice, looking quite disappointed, as she adjusted her posture and ran her fingers through her brownish-red hair. "I'm disappointed, I really am," she continued, as she took a cigarette box out of her expensive looking bag. She lit a slim cigarette and looked away, waiting for his response.

"Excuse my ignorance, but have we met before?" Marwan asked, beginning to feel slightly uncomfortable with the woman's demeanor.

The woman suddenly looked at him straight in the eye and changed her tone. "I am Farida El Leithy. I manage two TV channels. My time is money, and I have no time or energy to waste," she said emphatically.

"How can I help you, Madam Farida?" Marwan asked, still not knowing where this conversation was going.

"You better have full control over your people, Mr. Marwan. I hope you know exactly what you're doing with that police officer, Assem. If he doesn't control the situation immediately, blood will be spilled everywhere. It will get ugly. Very ugly," she said, with a threatening low tone.

"Who sent you here?" Marwan asked, getting angrier by the minute. He didn't want anyone connected with this operation to appear in his office, especially unannounced.

"I am here to tell you that my name is on that list too. We are in the same boat, and I know people who can take care of that woman if Assem fails to silence her," Farida said, exhaling a long plume of cigarette smoke.

"Of course not! The deal I have with my superiors is that Assem will handle the situation from the inside. He's one of the two main officers assigned to the murder case! How much more control can anyone have over the woman? Assem is shrewd and persuasive. Just give him time to do his job," Marwan said, purposely trying to lower his voice so his secretary wouldn't overhear them.

"I really hope you're right, Mr. Marwan! My only concern right now is to protect myself. We are both trying to protect ourselves here," she said in a sultry manner, stubbing out her cigarette with perfectly manicured red nails.

But Marwan knew from past experience never to trust anyone involved in the same operation. That's why he relished having his own private business, where he was his own boss, never obliged to share information or profit with others. That was also exactly why they chose him for this specific operation. He was a loner. A recluse. He fit the part to a tee.

Farida got up to leave, slipping her business card on his desk before she walked out of the office. She told him to call her immediately if he ever felt that Assem was losing control of the situation. But the young magnate knew better than to join forces with other members in the same operation. He only followed orders and instructions that were directly handed down to him by his superiors. That was how every operation was supposed to be managed. There were strict rules to be followed. Members rarely ever met unless something needed to be discussed or handed over in person.

Marwan looked out of his double-glazed window and watched as Farida got into her car. She was about to enter her black Mercedes when she briefly stopped and looked up, toward Marwan's glass window. She was certain she had left an impression on him and that he would be watching her leave.

Chapter Seven
'Overnight in Luxembourg'

He had just co-piloted a Boeing 737 into Luxembourg Airport and headed directly with his cabin crew to a nearby hotel. Murad had received a Code Red Alert on his phone the previous day, which meant there was no time for any error or delay. He had less than 24 hours to fulfill his mission and return back to Cairo the next morning. He was under so much pressure because he had just been informed that his own name had been exposed. He was working against the clock to ensure that all the names on that piece of paper wouldn't get leaked to the Egyptian police.

The meeting was to take place in two hours at Edmund Klein Park, in the heart of the city. Murad always chose to meet members of an operation in public parks, where he could easily blend into the crowds. He took a quick shower and slipped into a pair of baggy black sweatpants and a heavy hooded brown jacket. He then swiftly prepared his incognito backpack, which included a blond wig and a set of gray contact lenses.

Murad knew he was chosen for this operation for being a lot more than just an aviation pilot. He credited himself for being a master of disguise, knowing how to alter his appearance, accent, and demeanor depending on the mission that he had to accomplish. He ordered an Uber and quickly wiped his fingerprints off everything in the room before heading into the city. It took him under 15 minutes to reach a decent-looking café near the park, where he ordered his favorite *Paschteit* dish and washed it down with chilled apple cider juice.

He then paid his bill in cash, went to the men's washroom, changed his clothes, and donned his wig. He exited the café and walked for a few minutes before sitting on a side bench, where he discreetly wore his gray contact lenses and slipped on a cap. Changing appearances was one of Murad's favorite aspects of this job. He enjoyed the thrill of conning people into believing he was someone he wasn't.

Murad walked directly to the park, slowly changing his gait and faking a limp. He sat at the bench they had chosen to be their meeting point. He pulled out a small notebook from his backpack and pretended to be busy writing. An old man sat next to him on the bench and slowly unwrapped his sandwich. After he was done eating his sandwich, the man left the wrapper on the bench and got up to leave.

Murad looked at the wrapper closely without touching it. There was a message written in black ink. It read:

'Visit DD. It's been a rough time in Cairo. He will welcome you warmly, and you will walk away with memorable photos and gifts.'

Murad quickly understood what he had to do and left the park to go meet Demir Dogan, a photojournalist of Turkish descent residing in Luxembourg. Demir was a talented photojournalist who sold his photos to magazines and newspapers from all over the world. Murad had worked with him on two past operations, which were successful, but this message signaled that an operation had gone terribly wrong in Cairo and that Demir was needed for the swift cleanup. Demir was not only a talented photographer but an equally adept mobile phone hacker, whose services were invaluable in past operations. He had successfully managed to hack several mobile phones and retrieve sensitive information caches. He was also able to navigate the hidden world of the dark web, where he occasionally extracted valuable information for a hefty price.

Murad met Demir 10 minutes later in another nearby park, where they sat by the fountain area and immediately got down to business. Murad told Demir that his services were needed to rectify the mess that had ensued in Suite 55. He was ordered to provide all photos he had of Mona, the deceased victim, whom he had befriended, as they had previously collaborated together on two journalistic stories. Demir had wired several photos to Mona when she requested high quality-photos for her investigative articles.

The fact that his name was included on the list was reason enough for Demir to do all that he could to try to cover up Mona's murder. His life was in danger, and he knew he would most likely face the death penalty in Egypt should he be convicted and extradited. He told Murad that he had in his possession three digital photos of Mona, which were taken when they had met in Luxembourg to cover a human rights convention. Demir recalled how excited Mona was to be covering the convention and that she had joined Demir and a group of other journalists and human rights advocates for dinner one night. Demir understood that his mission was to professionally alter the three digital photos and hand them over to Murad by tonight. Murad's time was running out, and he had to take those photos back to Cairo the next morning.

But that was not all that Demir was going to hand over to Murad. The heavily built photographer casually opened his gym bag and took out a small white plastic bag, which he placed on the bench in between them. They agreed that the photos would be delivered in a package to Murad's hotel room by midnight, after which Demir got up and left the park.

Murad put the small white plastic bag inside his backpack, then headed to the nearest restroom, where he removed his contact lenses, blonde wig, and cap. He felt relieved to get the lenses out of his eyes, as they always left them red and irritated. He was even more relieved to be half way done with his mission in Luxembourg. He returned immediately to his hotel room to prepare his carry-on bag, laid it on the bed, and pulled out the small plastic bag from his backpack. He took out the medicine bottle he had brought with him from Cairo and proceeded to fill the empty capsules with the powdered substance he had just taken from Demir. Once back in Cairo, he was instructed to deliver the photos and capsules to Assem.

Murad's carry-on was almost never thoroughly searched whenever he checked into an airport, and the medicine bottle he used was a well-known over-the-counter brand, which never attracted the attention of airport security staff. Murad simply flashed his security pass with a confident smile and passed through the metal detectors. But it was the sniffer dogs that he feared more than the humans, even though he felt relatively safe this time because the substance he was going to carry onboard was what his superiors called 'an odorless base,' meaning that other hallucinogens would be added to it.

It was approaching 11 o'clock at night when Murad heard a screeching sound outside his hotel room. He remained silent as a brown Manila envelope slipped under his door. He picked up the envelope and carefully opened it with a pair of scissors, where he found three photos of Mona, as agreed. Demir had skillfully manipulated the shots, whereby the first shot showed Mona intimately speaking to a blond-haired man. The second photo showed Mona leaning toward the same man, while the final shot showed her leaving the restaurant with him.

The next morning, Murad wiped his fingerprints off everything in the room and headed to the airport. He passed through the special cabin crew metal detectors and entered the cockpit, feeling smug. His mission in Luxembourg was successfully completed. He now had to deliver these photos and 'gifts' to Assem. Murad knew that meeting Demir in person was very risky, but his superiors must have weighed the risks against the benefits. He also knew from past experience that members of an operation should never be trusted and that every member was in it solely for the cash, even though their lives hung in the balance.

Murad didn't want to continue working with the cartel for the rest of his life. He was beginning to ponder whether he should retire after this operation and move to another country to enjoy his newfound wealth. But he also knew that leaving the cartel would require an airtight escape plan. He would have to change his name and possibly alter his appearance for good.

As the plane took off, Murad thought about his past, how his parents were delighted when he became an aviation pilot, and how he would bring them gifts that made them overjoyed. But he also remembered how he was approached by a man in Cairo one day, who convinced him to carry small items from various destinations back to Cairo. At first, Murad didn't ask about what the small packages contained, but as his paychecks got larger, he understood that he was involved in something dangerous.

But it was too late for him to back out. He had gotten so hooked to the paychecks, much as the customers had gotten hooked to the 'red dust.'

Chapter Eight
'Catch 22'

Camillia left work at seven o'clock in the evening as usual and headed to the microbus station a few blocks away from the Imperial Hotel. She kept looking around her, fearing that she was being followed by the person who had sent her the text message earlier this morning. She pulled her headscarf down on her forehead, attempting to conceal her face from any onlookers, but her mind kept wandering to the list of five names that was tucked underneath her clothes in her closet.

Camillia began to wonder if she should head back to the police station and confess to Officer Maged that she had the list in her possession. She also kept wondering why, of all the rooms in the hotel, Suite 55 had to be the scene of this crime and why she chose to pick up the paper from underneath the curtain and put it in her pocket. She found it mind-boggling that this list could end up being the crucial piece of evidence in the murder case. She now felt that she needed police security more than ever, given that the perpetrator was blatantly threatening to take her life if she mentioned anything about the list.

She began debating whether to ride the microbus to her house or whether she should go directly to the police station to see Officer Maged. In the end, Camillia chose to go home, believing that it was prudent at this point for her to take the threat on her life seriously. She also wanted to check on her mother, who was still coughing incessantly despite the antibiotics and heavy doses of cough medicine.

Camillia boarded her usual white microbus and chose the seat behind the driver, clutching her black shoulder bag to her chest. The vehicle moved for about 15 minutes when a policeman at a security checkpoint stopped the microbus and asked the passengers to show their identification cards. She took out her card and handed it to the policeman, who then asked her to step out of the vehicle. Camillia felt self-conscious as she disembarked, while the other passengers stared at her intently.

"Camillia Sobhy?" the policeman asked after checking her ID card, all the while eyeing her with suspicion.

"Yes," Camillia responded, feeling uneasy with the way the policeman was looking at her.

"Let me see your bag," the policeman said, as he took the bag from her and began to search its contents. He opened the zippered compartment and pulled out a small white plastic bag, which Camillia had never seen before.

"What's this, Camillia?" he asked, with a tone that made Camillia's hair stand on end. She had never seen this white plastic bag before, and quickly realized that this situation was going to escalate into a living nightmare.

She began to hyperventilate, patting her chest and exhaling rapidly as the policeman opened the small white plastic bag, exposing a sachet of red capsules. He spilled a few capsules into his palm, while Camillia looked on in utter shock. He then opened one of the red capsules to find a white powdery substance, which he tasted with the tip of his tongue. He immediately radioed in for backup, then waved to the microbus driver, signaling that he could leave the checkpoint, while he took Camillia aside and told her to sit on the sidewalk until a police van arrived to take her to the nearest police station.

"I've never seen these capsules in my life, I swear, officer! Please believe me!" she cried in disbelief as she began to slap her cheeks repeatedly with both hands.

"Of course! That's what you all say when you're caught red-handed," the policeman responded, not showing much sympathy to her distress.

"I'm being framed! Please! My mother is an old, sick lady! I need to take care of her! I don't know anything about this! Let me speak to Officer

Maged right away! Call him, please!" Camillia pleaded as the policeman put handcuffs around her wrists.

The policeman looked at her with confusion; he was trying to understand what was going on. He had received a directive half an hour earlier to flag down this specific microbus and to arrest a woman on suspicion of illegal drug possession.

"Please! Officer Maged El Miniawy knows me! He questioned me this morning at the police station in *Zamalek*! He told me to call him if I needed anything. I have his number; please let me call him!" Camillia pleaded.

"I have to take you to the police station first where you're going to be questioned and possibly held for a few days pending investigation," the policeman said, as he began to feel some sympathy for the woman. After about 10 minutes, a black and white police van appeared by the curb. The policeman took Camillia to the van, where she sat near a curtained window, tears rolling down her face.

She immediately understood the reason behind this arrest, realizing that whomever had sent her the threatening message this morning had wasted no time executing this malicious act against her. She was being forced into silence and submission by the perpetrator. But little did the perpetrator know that this nefarious act had just strengthened Camillia's resolve to want to speak to Officer Maged and perhaps even tell him about the list. Another fact also hit her like a brick. Someone had planted drugs in her bag at the hotel today, the thought of which made her heart sink into a dark abyss. She wondered who could possibly do that in broad daylight at the hotel and quickly realized that it must have been someone with direct access to the housekeeping lockers.

Camillia's tears kept streaming down her face as the police van came to a standstill in front of the police station, where she was then escorted inside. Her body trembled as the policeman asked her to wait in an area designated for those awaiting interrogation. She observed the other people in the waiting area around her, finding that most of them fitted her stereotype of convicted criminals. Two angry-looking men were speaking and cursing at each other loudly, while three women sat huddled together with smeared mascara under their eyelids, heavy makeup, and excessively tight clothing.

After two hours of torturous waiting, a policeman approached Camillia and took her to a room where a police officer sat behind a black desk. The police officer asked her to sit down while another policeman picked up his pen to begin taking down her answers.

"Camillia, where did you get these drugs from? Are you a user or a dealer?" the police officer asked, looking at her straight in the eyes.

"None of these allegations are true! I have never seen these drugs before in my life! By the life of *Allah*! Please believe me! I'm being framed for something else entirely! I need to speak to Officer Maged El Miniawy, now please!" Camillia pleaded, her hands beginning to ache from the handcuffs.

"Where do you know Officer Maged from?" the policeman asked, obviously intrigued by the mentioning of another police officer's name.

"I was being questioned by him just this morning at the *Zamalek* police station. He will understand everything when I speak to him. I need to speak to him urgently, please!" Camillia begged.

The police officer left the room for about 10 minutes, during which Camillia kept sobbing loudly, feeling alone and terrified of the consequences of being charged with illegal drug possession. The police officer then returned to the room and continued his interrogation, asking about where she lived, her occupation, and her marital status. She answered all three questions, then asked about Officer Maged once again, at which point the police officer assured her that he had just contacted Officer Maged, who was currently on duty, and was going to speak to her very shortly.

Camillia let out a long sigh of relief and began smiling, feeling like a load had just been lifted off her shoulders. The police officer told her she was going to remain in the room until Officer Maged got a chance to speak with her. She nodded her head and looked down at her hands, still not able to fathom that she was being held in a police station like a criminal, handcuffed for the first time in her life.

The police officer left the room again, this time followed by his assistant. She was totally alone now. She stared at the clock on the wall, trying to think of who could have possibly put the drugs inside her handbag. She rested her head on her handcuffed hands and closed her eyes as images of her mother floated inside her troubled mind. She clearly understood that she was being framed to keep her mouth shut about the list of names she had found. She didn't know how the perpetrator had found out about the paper, unless he had accidentally forgotten it there.

After about 15 minutes of tortuous waiting, the door began to open slowly. She held her breath, hoping it was Officer Maged walking in to rescue her from this hellish predicament. She kept staring at the door and smiled when she heard a familiar male voice. She felt utterly grateful that her request to see Officer Maged had been granted so swiftly. She couldn't wait to tell him that she was being framed because of a list of names she had found in Suite 55. She wanted to free herself from an almost certain prison sentence and to return home to her mother.

But Camillia's smile suddenly vanished. Officer Assem walked across the room toward her.

He was smiling as he looked down at her.

Chapter Nine
'Murder Bytes'

Maged had barely slept during the past 48 hours, turning his office into a mesh of crime scene drawings, maps, timelines, and suspect profiles. He had solved the past three homicides in his career by using his uncanny strategy of fitting bits of information together as if he was piecing together a jigsaw puzzle. He liked to refer to his murder-solving strategy as *'murder bytes.'* The papers stacked on his desk led him to believe that the deceased journalist was killed in an unprofessional manner, likely to have been an unpremeditated murder. The evidence he had gathered from the forensics team during the past 48 hours suggested that something must have happened in Suite 55 that prompted the perpetrator to strike the victim repeatedly in the front of her head with a blunt object and then exit the suite quickly.

The forensics team had already examined the scene for blood spatter in the precise locations where Camillia had snapped photos on her cellphone. They tested for blood spatter on the wallpaper behind the bed as well as for traces of blood on the armchair. The only blood evidence found at the scene matched that of the victim; no other blood type or fingerprints were found anywhere in the suite. The fact that there were no fingerprints at the scene of the crime was a huge stumbling block for Maged, especially that material evidence such as sheets, blankets, and towels were removed from the scene, making DNA extraction much more difficult.

Maged was convinced that there was no sign of a physical struggle and that the victim entered the suite of her own free will, which begged the question of why she went up to the suite when her husband had testified that she was going to hand over her flash drive to the maître' D in the Indian restaurant. Maged watched footage from the hotel's CCTV, which showed the victim sitting at the restaurant and paying for her meal in cash. It does not show her handing over her flash drive, but Maged suspected that the flash drive was hidden inside the bills. He didn't understand why she went up to the fifth floor when that was clearly a dangerous situation for her.

He poured over camera footage of the victim inside the elevator and in the hallway leading to the suite, which showed her adjusting her clothes and entering the suite unaccompanied. It was clear to him that she was not being forced into the suite and that she was going to meet someone there, most probably to speak about the evidence she had collected for her explosive story. But what struck Maged the most was the fact that there was no footage of anyone else entering or leaving the suite, and no footage of housekeeping staff removing sheets or towels from the suite.

Maged repeatedly analyzed camera footage from the hallway leading to the suite, trying to see if any part of the footage had been tampered with or damaged in any way. His forensics visual and audio team scanned the footage several times, using specialized software for enhancement, but there was no evidence detected of a perpetrator entering or fleeing the suite, which greatly perplexed Maged. He soon realized that something wasn't adding up in the visual data. There seemed to be something he was missing. This was the first red flag that he needed to solve quickly.

Maged had also carefully interrogated the last guest who stayed in Suite 55. The guest was an Egyptian businessman who had meetings to attend in Cairo for two days before returning back to his hometown of Alexandria. Maged showed him photos of the deceased and asked him if he had ever seen her before, which the businessman emphatically denied. Maged also asked him if he had taken sheets, towels, toiletries or anything from the suite, which the businessman also denied.

The evidence thus far led Maged to believe that this was the professional cover-up of an unprofessional murder. The blood spatter that Camillia had seen in the suite was deliberately and professionally cleaned up before the forensic team had the chance to examine the scene of the crime. There were so many unanswered questions in his mind. First, how was the victim's body transported out of the suite without being captured on the camera footage? And second, why didn't the victim try to fight for her life. He was impatiently waiting to hear from the medical examiner, who was going to release his detailed report in a few hours. He hoped the coroner's report would give him the valuable insight he so desperately needed.

Maged also couldn't shake off the feeling that Camillia knew more than she was letting on, and he wanted to question her for a second time at the police station. She seemed to allude to knowing that Suite 55 was the scene of the murder before he had even seen camera footage of the victim entering the suite or even matching the blood type found in the suite to the victim.

He was about to ask a police officer to bring Camillia in for questioning when he backtracked and decided to go to the hotel the next day to question her there instead. He also needed to examine Suite 55 again, as well as the housekeeping detergents used in the hotel. Forensics had analyzed a patch on the carpet and found that it had been cleaned with a strong bleaching agent, the scent of which Camillia had told him she had picked up when she entered the suite. Maged needed to know if it was the same bleaching agent used by the housekeeping staff.

Maged's eyes were becoming extremely heavy as he looked at his pin board. He knew he had to take a break from pacing back and forth, as he finally sat down and let out a sigh of exhaustion. He just couldn't go on anymore without some shuteye, and he must have dozed off because he was awoken by his phone ringing. He sat up feeling energized, like he had been sleeping for days, when in fact he had been sleeping for only 14 minutes.

"Maged, I have some news for you about that girl, Camillia," Assem said, sounding agitated. "She's just been arrested for illegal drug possession. I came down to the police station here to see what was going on. She had asked to speak to someone from the Imperial Hotel murder case. I knew you were too busy in your office so I came down to see her," Assem said, as he lit a cigarette outside the *Boulaq* Police Station.

"Illegal drug possession? Just two days after the murder? That's awkward, don't you think? What kind of drugs? Did she confess or anything?" Maged asked, sensing a definite connection now between Camillia and the murder he was trying so hard to solve.

"She's denying knowing anything about the drugs, but you know how it is. They all deny knowing anything about the drugs, don't they?" Assem responded rhetorically.

"I was planning on interrogating her tomorrow about the murder. Now she's facing a drug charge too. There's no coincidence here, I'll come down to see her tomorrow, wherever she is," Maged said, sensing that he was closing in on something of major significance.

"No need, my friend. I talked to her, and she maintained her innocence. So, I convinced the police officer there to release her and put her under strict house surveillance. You never know; she could be our only link to the murderer," Assem said, stubbing out his cigarette and smiling to himself.

"You're right. I'm now surer than ever that she knows more than she's telling us. You did the right thing, but I still want to talk to her again. I want to keep her home for a few days, away from the hotel. I want to tighten the noose around her neck. She needs to feel cornered, and maybe then she'll break," Maged said.

Just then, Maged's assistant walked into the office holding a red folder. Maged hung up with Assem and took the folder from him quickly. His eyes were trained to scan such reports, only stopping when they needed to. He saw the words 'drug intoxication' and froze. The toxicology report showed that the victim had a concoction of illegal substances in her system. What struck Maged the most was the fact that this concoction was a novel one. He immediately put his 'murder bytes' together, concluding that the victim may have not fought back because she had been sedated by the drug.

It was beginning to look like the victim had gotten into some kind of argument with the person in the suite and that she was sedated by ingesting the drug in a drink or something. After being sedated, she was then violently struck by a blunt object on the front of her head. Maged kept picturing this scenario in his head, letting it play out repeatedly.

He now needed to know what type of drugs had been found with Camillia and whether or not the drugs were a match. In his mind, Camillia was now definitely a prime suspect in this perplexing murder. It was now his conviction that this murder had been carried out by a concerted effort and that it couldn't have been the work of one person gone astray. Maged was going to watch Camillia's every move once she was allowed to leave her house again.

Time was ticking against him, and the murder case was all over mainstream news and social media. He was under immense pressure to catch the killer fast. The people and the press wanted answers. International news agencies were hungry for any information, especially that the victim was a journalist. Everyone's eyes were on him and his police task force now. But his eyes and attention were now focused on Camillia. She either knew more than she was telling the police or she could be the key to solving this murder.

Chapter Ten
'Red Dust'

Marwan wasn't sure if the cargo container from the port of Antwerp had managed to escape the highly trained Belgian police force, which was on high alert during the past few days. The container was placed amongst 40 other chemical products, pharmaceutical, and metal containers to sail from the port of Antwerp to the port of Mersin in southern Turkey. The sailing time normally took 15 days, but Marwan wasn't sure if the container would actually arrive this time. Normally, once the container arrived in Turkey, it would then sail to the port of Port Said in Egypt, where Marwan's cargo handlers would be waiting to authorize the release of the container ship's cargo.

The system that Marwan had devised for the maritime transportation of the illegal substances from Belgium to Egypt had never failed him or his superiors before. Every person involved in the operation knew exactly what their role entailed, much like bolts in a conveyor belt. The substance was emptied into gel capsules and put into over-the-counter medicine bottles. The idea was a simple yet ingenious one. But the Belgian police force had been on high alert for the past few days, having arrested a large number of dealers by intercepting their Sky crypto-phones.

Marwan had never seen the illegal substance himself, but he knew it went by the name of 'red dust' on the market. He always tried to distance himself from getting too close to the substance itself, much preferring to let his handlers authorize and release the cargo to Assem's men, who then went on to distribute it to local dealers, mainly around the city of Cairo.

Marwan had been waiting impatiently next to his phone for the past three days, hoping to hear anything from the operation's team in the port of Mersin, which relied almost entirely on Demir's extensive contacts in Turkey. Once the container would dock in Mersin, encrypted messages would immediately be relayed to Marwan so that he could prepare his people in Port Said for the final leg of the journey. As the days dragged on with no word yet from Demir, Marwan found himself thinking of Farida El Leithy. He was curious as to what her role was in the operation. She had never disclosed that to him during their meeting. He wondered what her role was in this dangerous game of roulette.

He pulled out her business card and looked at it for a minute, debating in his mind whether to call her or to lay low. He was never a rash person, preferring to stay out of the limelight and watch others from the cool comfort of the shadows. Yet he felt a strange attraction to her, wanting to know why she would agree to be involved in such a risky operation. But his practical side always seemed to win him over, as he slowly put her business card back into his drawer. *"This was no time for emotions or risks,"* he told himself. His own safety always ruled supreme.

Just then, Marwan received an encrypted message on his phone. The container was due to arrive in the port of Mersin in three days. He let out a sigh of relief and dropped his head into his palms. The fact that the container had made it out of the Port of Antwerp was a miracle, given the tense situation in Belgium. He now had to prepare his own team in Port Said. This shipment was turning out to be one of the most difficult to handle, yet one of the most lucrative for him. He was eagerly looking forward to receiving a fat check in his bank account in the Cayman Islands.

But his superiors needed him to make sure that Assem had succeeded in controlling Camillia and that she would never be tempted or willing to divulge any information about the list to Maged. Marwan was aware that she had been arrested for the possession of illegal drugs and that Assem had convinced the police to release her, as she was now one of the main suspects in the murder case. Marwan was impressed with Assem's shrewdness, having ingeniously flipped the main witness in the case into the main suspect. But he wasn't sure if Camillia was willing to go so far as becoming the scapegoat for the murder, no matter how much Assem would offer her to remain silent.

Marwan became increasingly worried that the 'red dust' found in her bag would pique the interest of the police, as the substance was fairly new on the market, having been circulating in Egypt for only a few months. He was fearful that the fact that the shipment was due to arrive in three days in Port Said would be dangerous. Feeling increasingly agitated, Marwan got up to stretch his legs and began to pace around his office. He began to feel pangs of fear as he thought about the dangers of receiving the inbound shipment of 'red dust' at a time when the Egyptian police had just arrested Camillia with the same substance.

Marwan decided to head home and keep a low profile for a few days. He felt a deep desire to hide from everyone he knew and simply disappear out of sight. He waved to his secretary as he walked out the door, his dark sunglasses blurring his vision as he approached his car. Before he could start the ignition, his phone started blinking, signaling that he had received a text message. He read the message and let out his second sigh of relief of the day. It was an encrypted message from Assem informing him that he was trying to soften Camillia up so that she would keep quiet. Marwan started his engine and headed home, feeling a renewed sense of confidence about the success of this intricate operation.

As Marwan was driving home to his luxurious flat in downtown Cairo, Farida was trying to contact her superiors to inquire about her exact role in this operation. She knew that every name on the list would have to work double as hard to help cover up the murder in any way possible. They had told her to stay on guard as they monitored the progress of the operation, but she was getting increasingly irritated by each passing day. This morning was a game changer when she finally received a set of instructions. She was to pose as a friend of the deceased and to contact Officer Maged, offering to give a full testimony of what she knew about Mona.

Farida knew that her media relations and extensive social network made her the perfect candidate to pose as a friend and confidant of the deceased. She was instructed to tell Maged that Mona was consuming drugs and that she had advised her on several occasions to check into a rehabilitation center, but that the deceased had refused to seek professional help. Farida was to provide evidence that would lead Maged to believe that Mona had died of a drug-related murder in Suite 55, given that the coroner's report would definitely cite the drugs found in her system.

Farida's superiors were becoming increasingly confident that the operation was proceeding successfully, despite the murder. It was going to be one of the most intricate cover-ups ever executed by this cartel, which was eager to reap the profits of the 'red dust' shipment as well as succeed in covering up Mona's murder. Farida's role was a relatively simple one, provided that she carefully dug into Mona's past, extracting information that would lend credibility to her testimony.

She did exactly as she was told and spared no time in researching the background of the deceased journalist. She analyzed Mona's profile on Facebook and Instagram, trying to capture hints of her social interests and personality. She had to convince Maged that she was a close friend who knew intimate facts about Mona which other friends weren't privy to. Everything had to be airtight so that the police would suspect that Mona was consuming drugs in Suite 55 and that perhaps she had refused to pay for her fix, which in turn resulted in her murder.

Farida also had to keep track of Marwan, making sure that he was keeping in very close contact with Assem. The cartel operated in what is known as a 'circuit mode,' whereby every member of an operation made sure that the other was strictly fulfilling their obligations. Each member had to follow the exact orders given so that the operation proceeded seamlessly. Farida still didn't know who was tracking her, and that was how her superiors ensured allegiance and loyalty. It was an ingenious modus operandi devised to guarantee that members would always take orders from their superiors and constantly keep tabs on one another.

While Farida dug into Mona's past and social media accounts, Assem was receiving his instructions to follow up on Farida's testimony with

Maged. He was to make sure that she portrayed her role with conviction and that she would succeed in planting the notion that Mona's murder was a result of her addiction and involvement with shady characters. Assem was sure that Farida would make a credible witness and that she was pivotal to the success of this operation. Assem had never met Farida in person and was now instructed to meet her in a secret location where he would train her on how to give a convincing testimony. He was also going to provide her with details about Mona's private life, which could have only been known by a close friend.

Assem was well trained in digging up other people's dirt and equally adept at covering up his own. This new illegal substance was proving to be very popular among youth, and the cartel was adamant on making it the most accessible illegal substance on the market. Having learned from a young age not to get emotionally attached to people, Assem had only his own personal interest at heart.

He always believed in the audacious power of money, having been born into a poor family of eight children. He had left his small village in *Fayoum* and joined the police academy for only one reason. He craved power. He soon realized that power was almost always equated with wealth in this harsh, cold world.

The cartel gave him the wealth he so desperately craved. Coupled with being a policeman, Assem felt he could now conquer the world. He wasn't going to let anybody take that power away from him now. He was going to make certain that Camillia would be implicated in this murder if she gave away any of the names on the list. It was only a matter of time before the 'red dust' shipment arrived. His share of the profit was enough to make him consider early retirement.

It was only a matter of time.

Chapter Eleven
'Time Rewind'

Camillia felt numb as she sat on her bed, staring at the greenish-yellow mold stains peering down at her from her bedroom ceiling. She couldn't believe how her life had been turned upside down in a matter of just three days by this murder. Thoughts kept racing around in her mind, making her conclude that whomever had planted the drugs in her bag was the same person who had sent her the threatening text message earlier. She knew she was being blatantly forced to keep her mouth shut about the list of names which still lay tucked under a pile of clothes in her closet.

She got up slowly and pulled out the list to read the names once again. She surmised that the names must either be those of influential people or criminals of some sort, which made her certain that her life was now in ultimate danger.

She could hear her mother coughing in the bedroom across the hall, her breathing becoming heavier with every labored cough. Camillia didn't know how her mother would survive in this harsh world alone if she were to end up being murdered or jailed. Both outcomes would be unbearable to her sickly old mother.

But Camillia realized when Officer Assem proposed that she would stay home under house arrest for her own safety and that he would make sure her salary wouldn't be affected, that there was something amiss. He had convinced the deputy officer holding her for drug possession that she was a witness in a murder case and that she had to be kept in her home under strict police surveillance. Camillia, however, believed that there was something that didn't add up. She wondered if she was being framed for the murder or simply being forced to keep her mouth shut about the names on the list. She knew that both scenarios bode ill for her.

    She pulled out a small spiral notebook from her shoulder bag and began to write down all she could remember from the morning of the murder when she first entered Suite 55. She needed to trace back every detail very slowly, as if she were playing back a movie in slow motion. She began drawing bullet points all the way down the lined sheet, trying to create an orderly timeline for that fateful morning.

    She recalled entering the hotel through the backstreet staff entrance, then going to her locker to change into her uniform, and then heading directly to the fifth floor. She reached Suite 55 and entered using her black magnetic card, and immediately smelled the stench of a bleaching agent. She also recalled how the suite was really dark as the curtains had been pulled together, which is a strange thing for guests to do before they check out of a hotel room. Normally, at least in her experience, guests would leave the curtains wide open so that they could see their belongings as they packed their luggage. She also clearly remembered how all the bed sheets, pillowcases, towels, toiletries, and even the hotel's signature notepad and pen had been missing.

    She suddenly stopped writing as the image of an off-white shirt button laying underneath the oblong mahogany table came crashing to the forefront of her memory. She didn't report it at the time, but now she knew that every piece of evidence could potentially lead the police to the killer. She wanted to report seeing the button to Officer Maged, with whom she felt more comfortable speaking with. There was something about Officer Assem that made her feel uneasy.

    She continued writing, taking careful notes about the traces on the armchair and the rough stain she had seen on the carpet. Camillia then recalled entering the bathroom and finding all the toiletries and towels missing. She now also recalled seeing two small grayish hairs in one of the double vanity sinks, which would have most likely belonged to a male. She made a point to mention those two hairs to Officer Maged too.

Camillia couldn't remember anything else right now. She realized that she wouldn't be able to meet Officer Maged because she was forbidden from leaving her house. There was a policeman camped out in front of her building, watching her every move.

She pulled out Officer Maged's card from her bag and dialed his number. His phone was turned off. She began wondering whether she should just come clean about the list and have him protect her from whomever was threatening to kill her. *After all, he was a policeman, and it was the police's job to protect the innocent*, she thought to herself.

She began weighing the pros and cons of telling Officer Maged, as opposed to asking the person threatening her for a huge sum of money to keep her mouth shut. Camillia always had a feeling she would eventually make it in this world, but covering up a murder was never the path she had expected herself to take. She also wasn't sure whether the police would actually protect her from being murdered. She had no clue who was threatening her, but she did know that those behind the murder would have no qualms about killing again to stop their operation from being sabotaged by the police.

Camillia dreamed of a huge amount of money to get her mother and herself out of this crumbling apartment and into a more decent and safer neighborhood. But she had also always praised herself for being a defiant and resilient personality, one that never allowed others to intimidate or threaten her. The person who had sent her the threatening text message had somehow rubbed her the wrong way, and she debated whether she could perhaps play both sides against one another. She wondered if she could hint to the officer about the list and at the same time extort money from those threatening her. The more she told the officer, the more money she could demand from those threatening her. But she also knew that this dangerous strategy could backfire and that she could end up paying the ultimate price. She grabbed her phone and dialed Officer Maged's number once more, and was delighted to hear it ringing this time.

"Hello?" he said in a hurry, as if walking quickly somewhere. "Maged *beh,* I wanted to talk to you about some things I remembered seeing in

Suite 55 on the morning of the murder. But as you know, I'm being kept here at home. I need to talk to you as soon as possible," Camillia said, her heart pounding with every word.

"Ah, Camillia, I was going to come to your house to question you again after Officer Assem told me about the drugs they found in your bag," he said, his voice becoming harsher.

"No! I swear by *Allah!* I don't know anything about those drugs! Please come over to my house, Officer Maged. I won't be able to make more calls as my charging card will run out very soon!" Camillia said, feeling desperate to win the officer over.

She hung up feeling more at ease. She needed to have an ally who would protect her from those threatening her, and she instinctively trusted Officer Maged. He seemed professional and eager to solve this murder case as soon as possible, and she realized that it was in their best interest to collaborate together to solve the case. She knew he needed her information just as much as she needed the police's protection.

Camillia got up and walked over to where her mother was sleeping and sat down quietly next to her, feeling a sense of resolve. She looked down at her mother with pity, feeling determined to get the most out of this dire situation. She wanted to give her mother proper medical attention, and she equally wanted to fulfill her own dreams of living a more comfortable life. Camillia decided that if Officer Maged came to her house, she was going to tell him that she had received a sinister text message from a stranger who wanted her to stop speaking to the police.

She knew that Officer Maged would put her phone under surveillance and consequently put the killers behind bars. She believed that her phone was going to be the tool through which the police would be led to the killer. She now had to convince Officer Maged to get her a charging card, and maybe with time she would become so indispensable to the police investigation that they would forget all about the drug allegations that were being made against her.

Camillia knew she had only a few more hours to think very carefully about what she was going to tell Maged. She had already memorized the five names by heart and was now going to play the most dangerous game of her life. She had to decide which names she would reveal from the list. And with every name she would leak out to Officer Maged, she was going to ask those threatening her for more money to keep quiet about the remaining ones.

But something wasn't panning out the way she had planned. She wasn't receiving any more threatening texts on her phone. She now didn't know how she would use the blackmail card to her benefit. She wondered how she would even be able to ask for money if her phone was kept under surveillance. She felt stuck between a rock and a hard place; her plan didn't look like it would unfold the way she had desired. She was going to have to be patient and see if the perpetrators could come up with another means of communicating with her.

She was ready to commence a deadly gamble, but she was going to play the game with caution, much as she used to play chess with her classmates. She would win at times and lose at others. She understood that this was a difficult world and that her destiny had dictated her involvement in this murder case. She thought about how fate could have chosen any other housekeeper to enter Suite 55 on that fateful morning, but *Allah* had chosen her.

She randomly settled on the first two names she would expose to Maged.

Murad Abdel Hamid and Demir Dogan.

Chapter Twelve
'The Chameleon's Fate'

Murad woke up feeling more tired than usual after arriving in Cairo from his successful mission in Luxembourg the night before. He stretched out his body and began to mentally plan for how he was going to deliver the 'red dust' capsules and the photos to Assem. The handover had to be very well thought out, as his superiors had zero tolerance for errors. He was also becoming desperate to cash out his bitcoin payment into his crypto wallet, which was linked to his bank account in Zurich. His superiors had sent him instructions to meet Assem inside a specific cave at the *Zamalek Fish Garden*. It was a lush, green park where they could cross paths without attracting much attention.

The meeting was to take place at noon, a perfect time on a mundane Monday when most people would be at work. *The fewer the people around, the safer the venue*, Murad thought to himself. He sent Assem an encrypted message, which stated the time and place for the much anticipated handover. He wanted to give the seasoned police officer enough time to thoroughly prepare for this dangerous encounter. Operators were well aware that any type of face-to-face contact would be extremely dangerous, and Murad expected that a third party would be present as some sort of decoy. Surely enough, within the hour, Assem had responded back to him, confirming the time and place for the meeting.

Murad immediately prepared a grayish wig and a blue cap as props for his disguise. Having gotten used to manipulating his appearance, he owned several wigs, makeup products, caps, and glasses as part of his 'tricks of the trade.' For today's meeting, he was going to pose as a man in his fifties, possibly a middle-class bureaucrat, and he was going to carry a small leather shoulder bag, which would contain the bottle of 'red dust' capsules and photos of Mona.

He arrived five minutes ahead of time and sat down on a green bench near the park's main entrance. He pretended to read the newspapers as he waited for Assem to arrive. Ten minutes later, Assem, who was dressed in civilian clothing, arrived with another man, and they both walked into the designated cave. Murad waited ten more minutes before following the two men into the cave. When he arrived, the man with Assem had already left the scene. Murad had to make sure there were no cameras inside the cave before opening his bag. As if reading his mind, Assem slowly walked out of the cave after his trained policeman eye spotted a camera which was discreetly hidden behind the trunk of a large tree.

Assem walked to the back exit of the park, and Murad followed suit about 15 minutes later so as not to attract attention. They stood a few meters apart on the street and got into a nearby microbus. Once inside, Murad slipped the bottle of 'red dust' and three photos into Assem's plastic shopping bag. They didn't utter a word to each other. Murad left the microbus and walked for 20 minutes before stopping a cab. Assem remained on the microbus, and it took off two minutes later.

Feeling relieved that his mission had been successfully accomplished, Murad returned home, where he impatiently opened his laptop to check if his crypto wallet was showing any movement. There was nothing deposited into his account yet. He knew that bitcoin was a hassle to convert into cash and that his superiors used as few middlemen as possible to minimize any thwarts to their operations. He just kept telling himself to sit tight and to continue checking his bank account throughout the night.

About an hour later, Murad received an email alert on his laptop. He was always very cautious about opening emails from unknown senders. He was weary that these emails could be from hackers trying to infiltrate his email account and computer system. He didn't recognize the sender, but he could see that the email was encrypted and that it had an image attachment. His curiosity got the better of him as he clicked to open the email message. What he read made him freeze.

'Mr. Murad, you have been a great asset. However, we regret to inform you that you have been expelled. We received a photo of you which was taken discreetly by someone in Luxembourg. We expected nothing less than absolute precision. Monies owed to you have been retracted. Do not try to contact us.'

Murad was beyond furious and simultaneously scared. He was absolutely livid that after successfully delivering the capsules and photos to Assem, he would be so coldly axed from the operation. He was equally scared because he was almost certain that nobody had been following him in Luxembourg when he met Demir at the park. He wondered if this was the cartel's way of denying him his share of the profit immediately after he had delivered the goods to Assem.

Whatever the reasons, Murad felt betrayed by the people he had faithfully served and risked his life for. He knew that he was lucky to retain his job as a co-pilot, but the money he had made with the 'red dust' operation was making him afford a life he couldn't otherwise dream of. But he also knew that he couldn't utter a word to anyone. He had to remain silent because reporting anything would simply incriminate him. He was going to have to keep quiet and disappear for a while. Being expelled so abruptly meant that he might now be considered a liability and a threat to the cartel.

Around eight o'clock at night, Murad began feeling restless and overwhelmingly anxious. He decided to pack his wigs and all items he had ever utilized in his trade into a black duffle bag and dispose of them in a remote location. He packed his small backpack and decided to drive to his best friend's flat in *Ain Sokhna,* on the Gulf of Suez, where he would lay low for a few days. Murad kept a copy of the key to his friend's flat so that he could simply take off and unwind whenever he felt the pressure of life take a toll on him. He intended to dispose of the black duffle bag somewhere along the desert highway.

Murad made himself a tuna sandwich, turned off all electrical appliances in his flat, got into his green Jeep, and tossed his backpack onto the back seat. He glanced around the area to make sure that he wasn't being watched, murmured goodbye to the porter, who in turn nodded courteously, then drove off into the cold night. Murad's co-pilot instincts made him stop at a gas station to make sure his tires had the correct air pressure, and that he had enough fuel for the two-hour journey.

Murad couldn't drive his Jeep without having his favorite music blast from the speakers. He turned up the volume, buckled his seatbelt, and headed toward the Suez road highway. He enjoyed driving at night, much like he enjoyed flying at night. He never feared the dark; on the contrary, darkness gave him security, almost like a blanket wrapped around a cold, lonely child on a frigid winter's night. He kept glancing at his rearview mirror, making sure that he wasn't being tailed. Once he was certain that he wasn't being followed, his tense muscles relaxed, and he began searching for a flat deserted spot to dispose of his duffle bag.

Murad kept glancing sideways toward his right hand side, trying to spot some flat land amidst the desert backdrop. He began to slow down, making sure to turn off his headlights so as not to attract any motorists. He continued driving about a kilometer into the desert before finally coming to a standstill and stepping outside to bury his bag. He grabbed the shovel he had always kept in his Jeep and began to dig a pit in the sand. His muscles ached as he buried the duffle bag under a pile of sand. He then drove away feeling relieved that he had gotten rid of the evidence that could have linked him to the 'red dust' operation.

He turned his music back on and slammed down his foot on the gas pedal, making the tires screech in the night. Murad rested his head back and listened to the sound of his engine as it hummed through the night. He began thinking of how he was such a fool to have gotten himself entangled with such a dangerous cartel, but it was far too late to feel remorse now. He had just buried the evidence, and nobody would ever know anything about him except that he was a competent co-pilot.

He continued driving into the night. About nine kilometers later, Murad noticed a 4x4 vehicle approaching at high speed in his rearview mirror. He kept to the right side of the road, trying to make way for the speeding car to pass him by. But the car never passed Murad's Jeep. It suddenly swerved toward him, causing him to lose control of the steering wheel. He managed to regain control by putting his foot off the gas pedal. He had learned during his flight simulators to remain calm under stressful and unpredictable situations. But he knew this was no simulation and that more people died on the road than they did on flights.

The black Dodge rammed his Jeep again, with much more force this time. Murad tried to get a look at the driver, but saw out of the corner of his eye that he was wearing a ski mask. Murad completely lost control of the steering wheel this time, his Jeep flipping over three times into the sandy desert. His vehicle landed with a heavy thud on the hood, the impact immediately crushing his skull.

The Dodge slowed down so that the driver could make sure that he had succeeded in his deadly mission. Satisfied that he had completed his mission, the car drove off quietly, disappearing into the night.

Chapter Thirteen
'The Hourglass'

Maged woke up with nothing on his mind other than heading to Camillia's house to cross-examine her about what she saw in Suite 55, as well as the drugs that had been found in her bag. The past four days since the murder had been arduous and extremely stressful for him, with the media growing increasingly hungry for any information regarding the proceedings of the case. Maged was being constantly hounded for any leads about the identity of the killer, in a desperate attempt to placate the public's growing impatience and fear.

In Maged's mind, there was no doubt that Camillia was a prime person of interest, if not a prime suspect in the case. He felt that she knew more than she was telling him. He parked the police car under Camillia's building and exchanged a few words with the policeman who was keeping watch on her street. Bystanders looked at him and whispered to one another as he entered the old dilapidated building. He quickly went up the partially broken stairs, knocked twice, then waited impatiently, tapping his hands on the dirty, heavily scratched, wooden door.

"Maged *beh*, come in, please," Camillia said, adjusting her green head scarf to conceal her black silky hair.

"Camillia, I am here to ask you some straight-forward questions, and I expect nothing other than straight-forward answers. I want to get to the bottom of this quickly, and I know that you know more than you're telling me. This is your last chance to come clean," he said, looking her directly in the eyes.

"I will answer all your questions! I'm innocent, and I haven't committed any crimes! The drugs they found were planted in my bag to keep me silent!" Camillia said, hoping that she had made the correct decision to give Officer Maged two of the names on 'the list.' She had thought about it all night and decided it would be best to begin disclosing some of the names to Maged in exchange for witness protection. She wanted no one to be able to threaten her or her mother.

"Who is trying to keep you silent? You never mentioned anything about that to me when I questioned you earlier at the station!" Maged said, the adrenaline beginning to rush through his muscular body.

"I was scared! Someone sent me a threatening message on my phone, telling me not to mention anything about the piece of paper I found in Suite 55 on the morning of the murder!" Camillia stammered, the blood rushing to her face.

"What piece of paper? Why didn't you mention that to me before? Do you know what you have done here? I could charge you for withholding information and intentionally obstructing the proceeding of a murder case!" the officer shouted, blue veins bulging from his neck.

"I was scared! I don't want to lose my sole income! My mother is an old sick woman. I was scared to say anything!" Camillia said, her eyes welling up with tears.

"Show me that threatening message on your phone!" Maged demanded, reaching his hand out to take her phone.

"I deleted the message! I was afraid to be implicated in the murder!" she said, the tears now falling freely down her rosy cheeks.

"How can I even believe you now, Camillia? You're also denying knowing anything about the drugs they found in your bag! They're a match with the drugs found in the victim's body!" Maged said, feeling furious with her.

He wondered if she was playing him for a fool, thinking she could outsmart him. Camillia wiped the tears from her face with the back of her hand and told him that the piece of paper she had taken from the suite had about five names on it but that she could recall only two of them. When asked where the paper was, Camillia said that it must have fallen from her pocket the day of the murder before she had the chance to hand it over to security personnel. She then mustered all her courage and told him the names of Murad Abdel Hamid and Demir Dogan.

Maged shook his head in disbelief that she had kept this critical information from him. Before he could walk out of her flat, Camillia begged him not to mention the names to anyone else. She also pleaded with him to refrain from mentioning anything about the piece of paper to anyone working on the case and to move her to a safe location. She was terrified that the person who had sent her the threatening text message knew her current location.

"No! I won't have you moved to another location because if those threatening you already know your address and phone number, then it makes sense that you remain here under police surveillance. I want them to contact you again! I won't reveal what you just told me to anyone on the case, and I will send you another phone tomorrow, but don't you dare make any calls to anyone else," Maged said, as he opened the door to leave in a hurry. He was racing against time, and the information Camillia just threw at him had the potential to crack the case wide open.

"Thank you so much, Officer Maged!" Camillia said, feeling relieved that she could now get the protection she so badly needed.

"I need to trust you, Camillia! If you're lying, or if I find out that you're part of this crime, you'll be very, very sorry indeed," Maged said, as he looked at her directly, slamming the old wooden door behind him.

Maged rushed back to his police vehicle and immediately headed to the *Zamalek* police station. He entered his office and entered Murad Abdel Hamid's name into the national criminal database system. He found no matches. He then wired a request to the Interpol to run Demir's name in their database system. Feeling frustrated by the ticking clock on his wall, he didn't know how to narrow down his search for Murad, as many Egyptians have the same name. He began pacing back and forth, frantically clicking his ballpoint pen, as if by doing that he would miraculously speed things up.

But he didn't need to wait too long. Three hours after he began his frantic search for Murad's identity, a post on Facebook began circulating, garnering immediate media and police attention. A male body had been found by a motorist who reported seeing an overturned car on the Suez Road on the route to *Ain Sokhna*. The traffic police on the scene identified the deceased as Murad Abdel Hamid, a co-pilot employed by a national carrier.

Maged was astounded, and he wasted no time to call traffic police demanding that the body be sent to *Zeinhom* morgue for an expedited autopsy. He was extremely suspicious of the fact that Camillia had just disclosed the name of a man who was now found dead in an apparent car accident. *What were the odds of that being a coincidence?* Maged thought to himself. It was obvious to him that something wasn't adding up as he continued his search for the foreign man going by the name of Demir Dogan.

He googled the name and was dumbfounded when his search revealed a match. Demir Dogan was the name of a photojournalist residing in Luxembourg. Maged mentally connected the dots, linking Demir to Mona, whom he already knew was an investigative journalist. Maged felt he had suddenly made some progress on the case. He knew he had to find Demir as soon as possible and hastily wired a request to Interpol to bring him in for immediate questioning. Maged had to figure out if Murad and Demir were connected to each other and why their names were on the paper Camillia had found in Suite 55. He wondered how a co-pilot and a photojournalist living in Luxembourg could be connected to this murder case.

But what kept Maged wide awake that night was the fact that the drugs that were found in Camillia's bag matched the toxicology report from the coroner's office. He kept thinking whether Camillia was being framed to remain silent, as she had claimed, or whether she was somehow an accomplice in this murder. It was also becoming clear to him that Mona was either sedated by the drug in Suite 55 before being killed or that she was in the suite consuming the drug herself before matters somehow got out of hand.

Time was ticking against Maged, making him impatient and extremely eager to hear back from the Interpol, which had 18 databases full of information on criminals, fingerprints, and stolen passports. While Maged knew that all this information was accessible to countries in real time, he still needed Interpol to locate Demir and bring him in for interrogation. Demir's testimony was now pivotal to solving this case, so much so that Maged was willing to fly anywhere in the world to interrogate Demir in person, even though that would be impossible for him. Something in Maged's gut was telling him that this murder case was far more complicated in nature than he had previously expected. The fact that illegal substances were now thrust into the murder investigation gave Maged a new take on the entire approach to the case.

He was now trying to not only find Mona's murderer, but was now required to capture a ring of drug dealers as well. Maged knew that whenever drugs became implicated in a murder case, the investigation naturally took on a broader and more urgent national security dimension. Maged would now need the assistance of the national security sector and possibly one or two Special Forces units. He knew he would now have to bring out the heavy guns.

Camillia, however, remained front and center in Maged's thoughts. He was certain that her role in solving this case was far bigger than being a witness or even a suspect. He believed she may actually prove to be a major strategic pawn in catching the killer and possibly help bring down this dangerous drug ring altogether.

Chapter Fourteen
'The Making of a Witness'

Farida woke up and checked her phone for missed calls or messages. She usually silenced her ring tone when she wanted to get a good night's sleep, but this morning she woke up feeling very anxious. She was about to meet Assem for the very first time. He was going to explain to her how to give Maged a convincing testimony, and she knew she had to nail it in order to get the check deposited into her bank account. Her superiors had asked her to pretend to be a media mogul, when in fact she was nothing but a second-rate actress who never got the break she needed to make it onto the screen.

The cartel had chosen her, knowing that she could become whoever they wanted her to be. She may not have succeeded as an actress, but she surely felt that she made enough money conning people in the real world. That was fine with her, as long as she received her paycheck after her role was over. Today, she decided to dress in casual comfortable attire, and to listen very carefully to Assem's instructions. She relied on the belief that she was a fast learner and that impersonation was second nature to her.

They were going to meet at eight o'clock in the morning at an abandoned bunker along the Suez Road, where nobody would be in sight that early in the day. The thought of the meeting left Farida with little appetite for food on this dark and cloudy morning, but she knew she needed to have breakfast to ramp up her energy to absorb the information. She sliced a shiny green apple, being careful not to chip her red manicured nails. She checked the weather forecast and found that it was going to be a cold, rainy day in Cairo. She didn't like driving on highways in rainy weather, fearing the slippery roads, but she had no other choice. She had to follow the instructions.

Farida pulled out her black leather backpack and slowly packed in her phone charger, first aid kit, and pepper spray. Being a single attractive woman made her stay on the lookout for anyone tailing her.

She never relied solely on pepper spray for protection; instead, she had enrolled in self-defense classes for women, where she was trained to always expect the unexpected from attackers. Feeling satisfied that she was ready for her trip, she made sure all the windows in her apartment were securely locked before she headed out to her car.

The roads were slippery and wet as she had expected. She switched the radio to her favorite Arabic music channel before fastening her seatbelt and adjusting her rear-view mirror. Farida hated driving on highways, but this morning she was feeling impatient to get to the bunker and complete her task. She managed to get there 12 minutes ahead of schedule, giving herself enough time to find an ideal parking spot behind the bunker, where no motorists would spot it.

She entered through the back door of the shanty-looking bunker and found herself alone in a small space which had no windows. She was about to head back to her car when the green wooden door suddenly slammed shut, plunging her into complete darkness. She immediately reached for the pepper spray clipped onto her belt when she heard footsteps coming toward her. She instinctively ducked down in case this was an attacker coming at her.

"Don't worry, Farida; I won't hurt you. I'm here to help you, actually," she heard a male voice say, with a thick foreign accent.

"Assem? Is that you? Why is it so dark here?" Farida asked, feeling tense and very uncomfortable with the unfolding situation.

"I'm not Assem! The plan had to be changed. Your testimony has to be airtight, so they told me to come instead," the man responded.

Farida was puzzled and asked to see his face, which he immediately refused, saying that it was too dangerous for him to reveal his identity and that it would be safer for both of them that it remained that way.

"So why am I here then? Assem was supposed to meet me to give me inside information about Mona. What are you going to tell me about her?" Farida asked, feeling impatient and agitated.

"Actually, I can tell you more about Mona than Assem ever could. I can give you intimate details because I knew her on a personal basis. You've probably been pouring over her social media profiles, trying to paint an image of her that you could use with that police officer. I'm here to give you the information that will make you perfect your act with him," he said, sounding somewhat cocky.

Farida listened carefully as the mystery man told her details about Mona's mannerisms, her favorite cocktail drink, the way she preferred her cappuccino, as well as her burning passion for investigative journalism. He also told her the intimate secrets of Mona's relationship with her husband and how she had planned to get divorced after she was done with her assignment. He also told her that Mona was in an unhappy, unfulfilled marriage and that she was only staying in the relationship for the sake of her only son.

"Were you two more than friends?" Farida interrupted suddenly.

But she quickly bit her tongue, as she realized that her sole role here was to absorb the information he was feeding her. But that didn't stop her from secretly wondering how close Mona was to this mystery man before deciding that it wasn't her business and that she had to focus on memorizing the intimate details about Mona's life.

"When you speak to the officer, you have to look him in the eye every now and then. Don't appear too confident or that you have been rehearsing what you're saying to him. I hear that Officer Maged is very shrewd, and I assure you that he will see straight through you if you're not relaxed and natural. You have to seem genuinely distressed, and tell him that you had expressed your concerns several times to her husband concerning Mona's drug addiction," he said, his accent becoming more familiar to her ears now.

"What sort of drugs should I mention to the officer?" Farida asked.

"Good question! Tell him that Mona was trying out a new drug, going by the name of 'red dust,' and that her job entailed a lot of traveling to cover conferences and news events," the man continued with confidence.

"Is there anything else you know about her that I should know?"

Farida asked, feeling impatient to leave the dark enclosed place.

"Tell the officer that Mona had just recently hired a lawyer to help her with the divorce procedure and that her husband distrusted her, despite the deceivingly outward appearance of a happy marriage," he said, with absolutely no emotions in his tone.

The man's voice began to move further away from Farida, who was now able to see a little more in the dark, now that her eyesight had adjusted to the darkness. She could now make out the silhouette of a tall, heavy-built male figure wearing dark clothing and a ski mask.

"Good luck!" the man said. "Leave ten minutes after me," he instructed her. "And don't you dare repeat our conversation to anybody. Go straight to your house, and don't go out today at all."

The man disappeared quickly from a side door, leaving Farida plunged in near-complete darkness again. She waited for ten minutes as he had instructed her, then felt her way back to the door where she had entered. Once outside, her eyes hurt from the now sunny skies. She got into her car and sat there for a while in an attempt to calm herself down after this unnerving encounter before driving back to her house. Farida wondered why she had ever gotten herself into this messy business, shuddering when her hands clutched the cold steering wheel.

Meanwhile, the mystery man had jumped into the dark Jeep that had been parked outside. He got into the back seat and partially removed his ski mask to breathe more easily. The driver looked into the rear-view mirror and smiled before pressing the ignition button and driving away.

"Welcome to Egypt!" the driver said. "I never thought they would actually send you here," he said.

"*C'est la vie*! We never know what to expect in this dangerous job. One day they tell you to stay shackled in your home, and the next they ship you to another country altogether!" the man responded with exaggerated sarcasm.

"Take care of yourself, my friend. You're already on the wanted list. If they catch you, you'll pay a very high price," the driver warned in a solemn tone.

"D'accord! Merci Marwan. I will," Demir responded coldly.

Demir was totally against the idea of coming to Egypt in the first place because he had heard all about the skill and professionalism of the Egyptian intelligence apparatus. But his superiors, back in Luxembourg, had given him clear instructions to come to Cairo in person to speak to Farida so that she would be equipped to give Maged plausible and coherent information about Mona's personal life. He was counting the hours to leave Egypt and return back to his small, yet comfortable, apartment in Luxembourg. He wanted to go back to his own backyard, one which he knew as well as the back of his own rough hands.

He was used to living life in the dark, where he led a quiet life behind his state-of-the-art laptop, where he hacked websites and sometimes personal accounts in exchange for huge sums of money.

Chapter Fifteen
'Red Lines'

Marwan admired how ingeniously the cartel had managed to smuggle Demir into Egypt. They had hidden him inside one of the furniture containers that departed from Mersin port in Turkey to Port Said harbor in Egypt. Marwan's handlers were able to successfully foil attempts by the port's security personnel to open that specific container, and the fact that Demir had a dual Turkish-Luxembourgish nationality made it easier for him to move between both countries without attracting Interpol's attention.

Demir was told to come to Egypt for 48 hours to speak with Farida and to hide under Maged's nose. The cartel believed that the last place Maged would ever imagine Demir to be would be in Cairo. They were also expecting that Camillia would expose the names on 'the list,' which made them go to great lengths to keep team members protected until their roles had been successfully completed.

Now that Murad's name was crossed off their hit list, the cartel was in a cat-and-mouse game with the Egyptian police to make sure the container with the 'red dust' made it safely to Port Said harbor. With only 48 hours left until the shipment was scheduled to arrive, Demir had to lay low and return back to Luxembourg via Mersin, hiding inside a similar furniture container. The cartel favored Demir over anyone else in the operation, giving him the prized name, 'shadow man.' That was because Demir was their wild card. He was the one who was willing to do anything in order to rise in their ranks.

While Demir hid from sight, waiting to return back to Luxembourg, Maged was in close contact with Interpol, waiting impatiently to hear anything about Demir's location. The Interpol sent reports to Maged confirming that Demir was a resident and citizen of Luxembourg but that he was currently not in the country. The Interpol was also aware that Demir had Turkish nationality so he was placed on Turkey's 'watch list.' Maged was growing increasingly frustrated with the Interpol for not being able to find and question Demir.

Nonetheless, Maged was certain he was closing in on a huge break in the case and that he needed to make the connection quickly between Murad and Demir. He asked for Murad's last flight roster and felt he had hit the jackpot when he found out that Murad's last flight was from Luxembourg to Cairo the night before he was killed in the apparent car accident. Maged was now sure that both men knew each other, which made Demir's arrest an urgent necessity. Maged was also patiently waiting for the coroner's report on Murad's autopsy.

He opened his sketchpad and began drawing double-headed arrows with a thick red marker. He wrote down Camillia's name, then drew a double-headed arrow connecting Camillia's name to Murad. He drew a second arrow connecting Murad's name to Demir's. His third arrow connected Demir's name to Mona. His 'murder bytes' were now operating at full speed.

Five days had already passed since the murder, and he had still not presented the Minister of Interior with a specific list of suspects. But he now knew that this murder was a lot more complicated and darker than he had thought at the onset. The fact that the same drugs were found in Mona's body and in Camillia's bag made him certain that a dangerous drug ring was involved in this case and that Mona was killed because she was about to expose all those listed on the piece of paper.

Finding Demir was fast becoming his number one priority. Before Maged could continue his train of thought, there was a knock on the door. An assistant officer told him that a woman named Farida El Leithy was waiting outside to see him about the murder. She claimed that she had important information to offer to the police investigation. Maged told the officer to usher her in right away.

"Officer Maged, I would like to speak to you about what I know about Mona," Farida said, flicking her reddish-brown hair behind her back as she spoke with an air of confidence.

"Sit down. I'm all ears, Ms. Farida," Maged said, eyeing the attractive woman with some suspicion. He always trusted his gut instincts, and his hunch didn't feel very positive right now.

"I had known Mona—may *Allah* bless her soul—for a very long time. We had been very close friends since our college years together at Cairo University. We were both studying at the school of mass communication. She studied journalism while I chose media production," Farida said, looking down at her hands as if in deep sorrow.

"Why are you here, Ms. Farida? What can you add to our investigation that is of value? My time is limited," Maged said, feeling impatient already.

"I'm here to tell you that Mona had personal problems before her murder. I advised her to seek help for her drug problems, but she refused to do so. She was also going to seek a divorce after she finished her last journalistic assignment," Farida said, trying to look Maged in the eyes, as Demir had advised her to do.

"Do you know what drugs she was on?" Maged asked, his pulse quickening.

"She was on some kind of new drug. I remember the name because it was quite odd. It was called 'red dust,'" Farida said, sensing that her visit was making the impact she had intended it to.

"And what marital problems did she have?" Maged asked, remembering how he felt somewhat uneasy at the widower's apartment for some reason.

"She wasn't happy with her husband. She may have also been seeing someone else prior to her death," Farida added, looking downward as if in shame. "But of course, only *Allah* knows; God bless her soul; I wish she had heeded my advice," Farida said, looking away with crocodile tears in her eyes.

"I see. Do you have any idea why she was at the Imperial Hotel on the night of the murder?" Maged asked, hoping she had any clues to give him.

"She may have been there to take drugs from someone. The fact that they found her body near the hotel could signify that," Farida answered, looking at Maged directly. "Or maybe she was meeting her lover," she added, biting her lip in fake embarrassment.

Maged thanked Farida for coming forth with this information. She got up and left his office, swaying her hips as she walked away. Maged flipped open his sketchpad again and drew a fourth red arrow connecting Mona's name to Farida. He then looked closely at the red arrows and knew that he was closing in on something and that he was getting closer to making sense of this murder.

He believed that Farida's testimony warranted a second visit to Mona's husband. Maged needed to know if they were going to get a divorce prior to her murder and whether her husband knew that she could have been taking illegal substances. Just as Maged was about to ask the deputy officer to bring the widowed husband in for questioning, Assem walked into the office.

"Maged! I just received some important evidence in the case!" Assem said, his face almost lighting up with enthusiasm.

"What do you have for me today?" Maged asked, thinking that today may be his lucky day.

Assem tossed three photos onto Maged's desk. Maged picked them up one by one, his eyes widening as he carefully inspected each one. The photos clearly showed the deceased speaking to a blond man, then leaning toward him, and finally leaving the restaurant with him. Maged was surprised that these pictures surfaced today just when Farida El Leithy miraculously appeared at the police station to give her testimony. This coincidence gave Maged a very unsettled feeling. Once Assem left his office, Maged opened his sketchpad and drew a red arrow connecting Farida's name to a big red question mark. Maged believed there was an unknown person or entity at play here. There was someone always one step ahead of him. Someone who seemed to know which move he was going to take next.

It was becoming a game of mental chess, where Maged had to get all the soldiers and pieces ready to protect the queen from being killed. Camillia. As every moment passed by, Maged was certain he had to keep her under very close surveillance and protection. He needed to wait and see if the perpetrators were naïve enough to send her another threatening text message. But Maged knew they weren't going to attempt that move again. He was certain that those responsible for Mona's murder were also watching Camillia very closely and that they would devise unexpected tactics and strategies to eliminate her for good. It was now his job to see to it that their plans would be sabotaged by the Egyptian police forces. Nobody was going to be allowed to come near Camillia.

She was now becoming the key to unraveling this murder mystery. Maged knew he had to continue questioning her and probing further to 'jolt' her memory. Maged asked himself two questions out loud. First, *what if she were to remember more names*? Second, *what if she already knew about other names and was keeping them from him?*

Chapter Sixteen
'The Port'

Marwan had less than 24 hours to prepare for the 'red dust' shipment which was about to dock in Port Said harbor. He felt extremely nervous as he prepared his dinner, almost spilling his coffee all over his freshly pressed blue shirt. He was busy recording an audio message on his Sky ECC crypto-phone to make sure his team was prepared to handle the situation on the ground. This shipment was going to be his finale this year, as New Year's Eve was closing in and the 'red dust' season would come to a relative slow down.

Everything seemed to be in order, and Marwan began to relax a little, flexing his tense arm muscles. He looked at his Rolex watch and decided it was time for him to invest in a newer version. He spontaneously pulled out Farida's card from his wallet and decided to give her a call, even though he knew it was against operation rules. He dialed her number and waited impatiently for her to pick up, but she never answered. He felt ashamed of himself and immediately regretted what he'd done. He stretched his legs out and laced his hands behind his head. Five minutes later, he received a phone call.

"Hello, Mr. Marwan. What a surprise! Is everything alright on your end?" Farida asked in a sultry tone.

"Yes, Ms. Farida, all is well. Is all well at your end too?" Marwan asked, pretending that it was a mere business call.

"Well, yes. You know I can't talk much. Would you like to meet somewhere secure?" she asked.

"That would be great! Perhaps after tomorrow when everything is settled here, *Inshallah*, the way we all hope it will be," he answered, hoping she understood his coded message.

He hung up, feeling confident and somewhat smug. He was attracted to Farida but feared the repercussions of getting emotionally involved with an operation member. *But if she kept silent about their relationship, the cartel would never find out about it*, he thought to himself.

Marwan then received a coded message on his secure line from Assem. The officer was inquiring about the exact timing of the shipment so that he could prepare his men for the port handover. The handover had to be airtight, with no errors or a single mishap. Both men were well aware of that. They both also knew how to operate in flawless sync together, but were very fearful of what may happen if this particular shipment got derailed or impounded.

Over at Port Said, Assem had planted a team of four men who were dressed as port handlers, with falsified identities and name tags. They eagerly awaited the container ship from Port Mersin in Turkey to dock safely. Marwan's handlers were also in place and ready to complete their part of the operation. Assem had arranged for a helicopter to escort the incoming container ship until it docked, under the pretense that the port needed air surveillance to ensure that ships wouldn't collide or block entry to the busy port.

While Marwan and Assem were coordinating their efforts in preparation for the incoming container ship, Demir was on his way back to Port Said, riding in the backseat of a private black sedan. He wore dark sunglasses and a thick olive green sweater, trying to look as inconspicuous as possible. With less than 24 hours left for him to escape back to Turkey, he was becoming nervous. He was wary of the checkpoints on the road, but was ensured that with a diplomatic license plate, he would be able to evade being stopped by traffic police. Demir was extremely anxious to get out of Egypt for fear of being detained or implicated in Mona's murder.

He began to recall how she was so eager to be the best investigative journalist in Egypt and how she was always warm and friendly with other journalists whenever she attended conferences in Luxembourg. She had once told him that she was about to release an explosive story in Egypt, and he immediately relayed this information to his superiors. They instructed him to befriend her in order to find out as much as he could about her personal life. Mona told him over lunch one day that she was having marital issues and that she was contemplating a divorce. Demir, having learned not to have sympathy for anyone earlier on in his troubled childhood, simply listened intently, unable to offer solace to the distraught woman.

He was so deeply absorbed in his memories that he failed to notice the checkpoint coming up. The traffic police officer wore a thick black sweater underneath a leather black jacket. He waved his hand for the car to stop, and Demir suddenly felt a lump form in his throat. He was assured by Assem that the car wouldn't be flagged down because of the diplomatic license plates. His heart began to race wildly, and he was finding it difficult to control his breathing.

"The car's license and yours too," the policeman coldly told the driver, as he peered at Demir in the backseat. The driver produced the two required licenses, while Demir looked the other way, trying to be as composed and nonchalant as possible, but he couldn't help interlacing his fingers together nervously. The policeman checked the licenses, then courteously nodded his head and waived for the car to pass through. Demir let out a sigh of relief, feeling even more desperate than ever to get to Port Said harbor.

It was getting dark, and the weather was colder than usual for December in Egypt. Demir shivered and longed to be back in the safety of his small apartment in Luxembourg. He began to wonder what his life would have been like had he chosen to simply be a photojournalist. He was getting tired of being part of the cartel, despite the huge amounts of money he was making. He began to crave the luxuries of a layman – the simple everyday normalcy and boredom. He didn't want to keep looking over his shoulder anymore. But he knew how important he was for the cartel and how they depended on him as their liaison between Europe and Egypt.

Port Said was now only half an hour away, and the 'shadow man' began to slowly let his guard down. He received a text message from Assem inquiring about his exact whereabouts, and he immediately responded with a live location message. Demir took a deep breath as the black sedan entered the busy *Gomhuriya* street in Port Said. Street vendors were still selling their products on the pavements, several of them looking at the black car as it passed them by.

The car made its way to the port and was granted clearance to enter through the security gates. The vehicle was stopped by two port handlers wearing hooded orange overalls with silver strips that shimmered in the dark. One of them told the driver to continue toward the wharf, where a Turkish container ship was docked. Once the car came to a halt, Demir exited the vehicle and was led to the accommodation section of the container ship, adjacent to the main mast. There he was greeted by one of the cargo handlers, who led him to a sleeping chamber. It was a small space, but it sufficed for Demir to stretch out his tall, well-built physique.

The cargo handler gave Demir a plate of food and a bottle of cold water, after which he shut the door. Demir was hungry, cold, and extremely claustrophobic in this small space. He nibbled at the bread and piece of white cheese on his plastic plate, then drank almost all of the water in the bottle. He rested his head on the pillow, staring at the white gypsum board ceiling and desperately wanting to drift off into a deep sleep. He began to feel more secure now, thankful that his superiors had left him in safe hands, as he curled up into a fetus position and fell asleep.

Six hours later, Demir was woken up by the sound of helicopter rotor blades. He tried to sit up, but his head felt heavy and his heart was beating wildly. He was now sure that the container ship with the 'red dust' was about to dock at the port and that Assem had secured a helicopter to ensure safe entrance into the port. He was told that once Assem and Marwan's men were able to get the 'red dust' out of the port safely, his container ship would begin sailing back to port Mersin. Everything had to be in perfect synchronization. There was no room for error.

Demir was repeatedly informed that the Egyptian police were probably already tracking them all down. He had to get to Turkey immediately and hunker down for a few weeks before attempting to return to Luxembourg.

There was a sudden knock on his door. A gray-haired man walked in, dressed in a gray crumpled suit.

"How are you, Demir? We need to talk," the man said, looking at Demir with cold, almost inhuman eyes.

Demir froze.

He had never seen this man before, and he didn't like his business-like, matter-of-fact attitude. But more importantly, Demir was never given instructions to speak to anyone other than Farida and Marwan on this trip. Demir believed that the mere fact that this man had managed to make his way into his cabin was a clear signal that something was very wrong.

In fact, Demir was certain that this was going to be his last conversation with anyone.

Chapter Seventeen
'Camillia's Gambit'

Camillia was growing more impatient by the hour. She was still staying at her flat in *Boulaq* with her mother, having not heard from Officer Maged for the past two days. She hadn't slept since then, trying to decide whether she should disclose one or two more names to secure herself witness protection status. She hadn't received any more threatening messages on her personal phone and was using the other phone that Officer Maged had given her instead. She desperately needed money to pull herself out of her financial rut, but she wasn't going to mess with the police either. This was a murder case, and she opted to keep herself and her mother safe.

She pulled out the piece of paper once again and looked at the remaining three names. She had to come up with a credible scenario to convince Officer Maged that she managed to remember a third name. She wanted the officer to consider her an indispensable witness. She believed that the more pivotal she became as a witness in this case, the more she would secure her safety and her irrevocable exemption from the drug charges that the police had levied against her.

She was about to call Officer Maged to disclose the third name to him when she heard a loud knock on the door. Her body stiffened. Her mother called out to her, telling her not to let anyone other than Officer Maged into the apartment. The knocking became louder and more impatient.

"Open the door, Camillia! I'm Officer Assem," she heard the officer say in a harsh tone.

Camillia went to the door and opened it quickly. She wasn't fond of the officer, feeling somewhat unnerved whenever she looked into his glassy brown eyes.

"Of course! Come in," Camillia said, trying not to meet his gaze.

"I'm here to see if anybody has bothered you or threatened you in any way since you were put under house arrest," he said, his eyes roaming around the flat.

"I already spoke with Officer Maged. He was here two days ago, and I told him everything I know," Camillia said, her knees becoming shaky.

"Well, I'm here to hear it too! What did you tell him?" he asked, his eyes glaring with a sort of unforgivable wrath.

"I agreed with him not to speak to anyone about the case. He agreed to that," Camillia responded, feeling more uneasy by the minute.

Assem took a few paces around the small living area and came really close to Camillia. She took two steps back and was pinned against the dirty gray colored wall. She was stricken by an indescribable fear as she looked into his dark eyes. She shuddered and looked away.

"Camillia, remember that I am the one who brought you back to your apartment to keep you safe after you were charged with illegal drug possession. You can trust me too! I am working with Officer Maged on this case. I need to ask you again if you remember seeing anything in Suite 55 that can help us?" the officer asked, calmly lighting a cigarette from a crumpled Cleopatra cigarette pack.

"I need to use the bathroom, Assem *beh*," Camillia said, walking away hurriedly and tugging at her headscarf.

She locked the bathroom door behind her and texted Officer Maged quickly, asking him if she should disclose anything to Assem. Maged responded immediately, instructing her not to reveal anything new to him. She walked out of the bathroom looking calmer and more composed as she told Assem that she had nothing new to add to her testimony except that she was fed up with being locked up in her apartment.

Assem looked at her intently, sensing that she was hiding something. He puffed out the cigarette smoke directly in her direction and took a few steps toward her again.

"I will keep you safe too, Camillia. We need to solve this case as soon as we can. I told your boss at the hotel to pay you your salary, even though you don't go to work anymore. I'll be back in a day or two to hand you your salary myself, and if you need extra cash, don't hesitate to ask me," Assem said, smiling at her as he showed himself to the door.

Camillia caught her breath as Assem shut the door behind him. She called Maged again and told him that she needed to talk to him. He told her he would call her back in half an hour. She knew that keeping the names on 'the list' from Maged would get her nowhere now that her personal phone line was not receiving text messages or any phone calls. She also knew that the people threatening her were not naive enough to text her again directly, meaning that she would no longer be able to play both sides in order to extort money out of the situation. She concluded that her only way out of this murder case was to align her interests with Maged and to eventually disclose the remaining three names to him. But she feared that Maged wouldn't believe that she had suddenly remembered a third name. But she decided to disclose Farida El Leithy's name anyway. She believed that the fact that Farida's name was somewhat familiar to the public would make matters more credible to the officer.

"Camillia!" her mother called out, coughing sputum out loudly. "*Hajja*, I'm sorry I haven't been sitting next to your bed as I usually do. My mind is really preoccupied now," Camillia said, as she held her mother's cold hand.

"What's happening? Camillia, are you keeping things from me?" her mother asked, her fingers becoming increasingly crooked as her arthritis progressed.

Camillia explained to her mother that she had to comply with everything the police told her to do in order to protect them both from harm. Half an hour later, Camillia's phone rang. Maged sounded very impatient as he asked her about what she had wanted to tell him earlier.

"I think I remembered another name today! I remembered it because I heard it being mentioned on a television show this morning," Camillia said, not sure she sounded very convincing, even to herself.

"What name? Tell me quickly, I'm racing against the clock here," Maged said, his gut instincts telling him he was right all along not to trust this deceptive woman.

"It was the only female name on the list. I think the name was Farida. Farida El Leithy. Yes! That's it, Maged *beh*," she said, her heart beating furiously as she waited for his reaction.

Maged was incredulous when he heard that name being mentioned. *What were the odds of Farida El Leithy's name being on that list in Suite 55?* he thought to himself. Farida had just willingly gone to the police station to give her testimony. The officer opened his sketchpad and looked at the names and the thick red arrows that he had just drawn only hours earlier. He began to wonder again how Farida, Murad, and Demir could be all tied to the victim. With Murad turning up dead and Demir having vanished into thin air, it looked like Farida had to be arrested quickly before it was too late to question her again.

Maged called his two deputy police officers into his office and gave them instructions to arrest Farida El Leithy and bring her in for immediate questioning. He knew there was something very dangerous happening here and that the list of names may be turning into some sort of target hit list, proving pivotal to the investigation. He wholeheartedly believed that Camillia was the key to solving this murder. With every name she revealed to him, he felt he was getting closer and closer to identifying Mona's killer. But something told him that those behind Mona's murder were very well organized and that they were also very well connected. *Perhaps too well connected*, he surmised.

He laced his hands behind his head as he began to feel that this case wreaked the modus operandi of an international drug cartel. A drug cartel that was dealing in 'red dust' and highly connected in Egypt. He knew he was up against international drug lords and that he had to ramp up his investigating team and prepare a large squad of policemen for this case. He knew he was going to need the help of more than one Special Operations Unit. Maged now truly believed that this was not a murder where the deceased was consuming the 'red dust' herself, nor was it the work of a jealous husband who found out that his wife was cheating on him. He was now certain that Mona was killed because she was going to expose an international drug cartel, one that was highly experienced in organized crime.

Maged began pacing the room back and forth as a mental clock continued to tick incessantly inside his head. He reached for his secure landline and called the Minister of Interior's bureau. He was going to have to take this case to the highest level.

It was now a matter of national security. It was time to launch the 'dragnet.'

Chapter Eighteen
'Day 7'

Farida was looking forward to meeting Marwan sometime today, assuming that the shipment of 'red dust' had arrived safely at Port Said harbor and that Assem had successfully secured the handover. She knew she wasn't allowed to have personal connections with anyone involved in the operation, but she was also tired of fighting against this cold world on her own. She perceived Marwan as a viable, single, and affluent businessman, making him the perfect mate for her unyielding ambitions. Even though marriage wasn't something Farida aspired to, she was all in for the idea of having him provide for her, in whatever shape or form the relationship would take. She also knew that it was going to be a huge risk, given how the cartel kept them all under very strict surveillance, as if they were all rats under a massive microscope looming above their heads.

She had done her part and gone to Officer Maged, giving him all the details that she was told to give by the 'mysterious man' who had vanished into thin air. She remembered his attractive thick French accent and began to wonder where he was from, and how he was connected to Mona. She quickly dismissed those thoughts and began to focus on how she would spend the big amount of money that should have been deposited by now in her bank account in Zurich. She opened her laptop and checked to see if the amount had been deposited, but found that there was nothing appearing on her balance yet. She knew bitcoin transactions took a bit longer than the traditional system of transactions, so she decided to be more patient.

She stared at herself in the mirror and wondered how her pitiful life had ended up so complicated and entangled. She wondered whether she would ever have a normal life and be able to walk the busy streets of Cairo without being on the lookout all the time. She acknowledged the mayhem and havoc that this powerful cartel was capable of doing but she also enjoyed the money she was making. It was a burden she was going to have to learn how to balance throughout her life. But one day she hoped she could free herself and leave to a country where she would be unknown and unwatched. But with such a powerfully connected cartel, Farida wondered if there was any country in the world that would be safe enough for her.

Farida received an encrypted text message on her phone. It was a message from Marwan telling her he was ready to meet her today at three o'clock at a secure location on the Suez Road. But he made the strange request that she disguise herself in a *niqab* garb, just in case she was being followed by the police or anyone from the cartel. Farida now suddenly felt both excited and apprehensive about this meeting. She began to think about what she would wear underneath the *niqab* outfit to further seduce Marwan. Her heart began racing as she began to think of what could happen in this meeting. As much as she longed to be free from the cartel's control, she also loved the addictive danger that came with it. It was a danger she wanted to shake off, but at the same time, she thoroughly enjoyed the adrenaline rush.

Back at Port Said harbor, the container ship with the 'red dust' had docked safely parallel to the wharf as port handlers busily unloaded the cargo. Assem was coordinating every move from Cairo, using his Sky crypto-phone, making certain his audio and text messages would self-destruct exactly two minutes after they were heard by the receiving party. The two 'port handlers' in disguise had seized control of the illegal substance with the help of Marwan's cargo handlers and had discreetly left the port using the safe exit that Assem had provided.

As instructed, the two men had found the black sedan with a diplomatic license plate number parked in a relatively secured spot. They quickly got inside the back seat of the vehicle and changed their orange, soiled overalls. A dark gray duffle bag on the back seat contained two pairs of pants and two shirts, as well as two fake diplomatic passports and ID cards. The two men had now simply taken on the persona of two diplomats from Turkey, returning back to Cairo after having checked the operational and managerial standards of Port Said harbor. After all, Turkey was one of Egypt's main export partners, and so there would be no reason for police suspicion.

As the black sedan was driving off, Demir Dogan sat up in bed, trying to straighten his upper body as he looked into the cold eyes of the gray-haired stranger who had just entered his small room. He felt a strange, foreboding sense of fear.

"Who are you? I wasn't instructed to speak to anyone," Demir said, his gut telling him to be careful with every word he uttered.

"Plans have changed, Mr. Demir. You know how it is with us. We control the pace, and we set the modus operandi. It's all in our hands," the man said coldly, as he sat at the foot of the bed, his poker face giving nothing away.

"What do you want to know? I don't speak about any details to anyone. I do as I'm told, and I don't ask any questions," Demir said, feeling like a cornered prey in the tiny claustrophobic space. He felt strangely exhausted, and his eyelids felt like they weighed a hundred tons.

"You are an excellent informant and a very valuable asset to us. But, unfortunately, my friend, your name has been on Interpol's watch list for the past three days. Your name was leaked to the Egyptian police, and of course we know exactly who leaked your name. We can assure you that the woman will pay dearly and we will exact our revenge in due time," the man said, looking directly into Demir's tired looking eyes.

"You endangered yourself to come and tell me this? You could have sent that to me by encrypted text," Demir said, as his tongue began to feel heavy and his muscles felt weaker with every passing minute. He didn't feel right this morning. He almost felt like he was under some sort of sedation.

"We value our people, Demir. I had to look you in the face and pay my respects. Our respects, as a matter of fact. On behalf of our organization," the man said, as he straightened his crumpled jacket and got up to leave.

"I don't understand," Demir said, as he lay his head back on the pillow.

He didn't have the energy to sit up anymore. He began to feel paralyzed in his own muscular body. His eyesight was becoming blurred, no matter how hard he tried to squint or focus on something. Images of his father began to float around in his mind. He could see the rusted silver buckle of the brown leather belt gash his forehead repeatedly, and how he had to stop himself from crying so that his abusive father wouldn't beat him over and over again. He wasn't allowed to cry or show any emotions. He was taught that emotions were a sign of weakness. He had to become numb to survive.

That was the last thought Demir would ever have. His body became lifeless after exactly 23 minutes. He lay curled up in a fetus position, leaving this world just as he had arrived.

Alone. Unwanted. Neglected.

The container ship carrying Demir's body began to sail away from Port Said harbor to Mersin port in Turkey, where Demir's body was then bagged by the cartel's port handlers and discreetly disposed of in his own homeland. The process was executed coldly and quietly.

Nobody would ever find Demir Dogan again.

Chapter Nineteen
'The Dragnet'

Maged had slept six hours in the past two days. His mind was racing against the clock as the pressure was continuously building up, becoming more and more unbearable after one whole week of continuous around-the-clock investigations, collaborating with Interpol, and questioning a multitude of secret informants. The seasoned police officer finally decided to head to the bureau of the Minister of Interior with a complete portfolio on the Imperial Hotel murder case and the connection it had with what he believed was a nefarious international drug cartel operating overseas.

The police officer's mission was to convince the minister that he had gathered enough evidence and probable cause to form one of the largest dragnets in the history of the country. Maged wanted to bring this cartel down, not only cutting off all its operations within Egypt but also cutting off its poisonous tentacles from the entire world. He knew he had to have solid evidence in his possession, but he also knew that the Ministry would back the dragnet with whatever means necessary. Maged now considered this case to be a matter of national security, and he expected the secret service sector to become part of the powerful dragnet, one he was so desperate now to create.

Maged walked with a confident stride as he approached the grand column façade of the Ministry of Interior building. He was met by one of the minister's aides and was hurriedly ushered into the main boardroom. Maged had his laptop bag slung over one shoulder and two red folders in the other hand. He quickly put everything down on the long mahogany meeting table and shook the minister's hand. There were three other officers and high-ranking security personnel in the room. This wasn't solely a murder case. It was a murder case associated with an international drug cartel that was smuggling one of the most potent and lethal new drugs into the country.

"Sir, I am so grateful for your time. I know your time is extremely tight, but I had to bring all my evidence to you myself and to explain why I am proposing such an extensive involvement of manpower and intelligence personnel," Maged said, pronouncing every word emphatically and with solid determination.

"Officer Maged, I've been closely following everything about this case, but I would like to hear your most compelling evidence. I have no problem with securing necessary police manpower and making sure we work very closely with the national security sector," the Minister said, with a commandeering voice, giving Maged reassurance and confidence to proceed.

"I have been collecting evidence diligently for the past eight days, and I have come to the conclusion that an international drug cartel operating overseas is smuggling a new drug, going by the name of 'red dust,' into the country," Maged explained, as the digital maps in the boardroom lit up along one wall.

Maged got up and walked over to the digital interactive maps, clicking on Egypt, Turkey, and Luxembourg. He enlarged the three map locations using his pointer finger and thumb. The Minister and his aides watched intently as Maged was about to present the most important case of his career.

"There is a link between two individuals, who were both mentioned on a piece of paper found in Suite 55. I believe both men are working with the cartel. The first suspect is an Egyptian co-pilot named Murad Abdel Hamid, who died in a car accident only one day after returning on a flight from Luxembourg. The second man is Demir Dogan, a photojournalist with a dual Luxembourger-Turkish nationality. We cannot locate this man, and the Interpol has come up with no leads thus far," Maged explained, drawing a red line with his pointer finger between Egypt and Luxembourg.

"What makes you believe that the two men are connected? Could it not be circumstantial?" one of the minister's aides asked.

"I believe not, given that we have evidence that Demir knew the victim and that they had met previously in Luxembourg during a human rights conference. I believe that Murad was transporting small doses of the illegal drug into our airports and that he was also a liaison of sorts, carrying important documents into Egypt," Maged continued. "I also have the name of a female, Farida El Leithy, a second-rate actress who joined the cartel, after which she posed as an affluent media personality. We are trying to locate her and bring her in for further questioning as we speak," Maged said, his eyes now glued on the minister's facial reactions.

"How is Farida implicated in all this?" the Minister himself asked, looking directly at Maged.

"Her name was also on the list found in Suite 55. She came into the police station three days ago, claiming that she was a close friend of the deceased, trying to convince me that the victim could be a drug addict. The toxicology report did indeed conclude that the drug, 'red dust', was present in the victim's blood. Farida also alluded to the notion that the victim may have been having an extramarital affair," Maged answered with confidence. "To my surprise, Assem handed me photos of the victim in which she was accompanied by a foreign-looking man in Luxembourg, on the very same day Farida gave her testimony!" Maged said, his sharp mind working quickly to put the pieces of the puzzle together as eloquently as he could.

"How did Assem get those photos?" one of the minister's aides interjected quickly.

"He said they had been delivered by postage to the police station. I verified that they were indeed sent by mail. But they were mailed from within Egypt," Maged affirmed. "Which makes me believe that Murad could have brought the photos with him on his last flight from Luxembourg. I also believe that Murad was killed by the cartel because his role was successfully completed in the operation. So it is very possible that the cartel had him killed off in what seemed to be a car accident on the Suez road," Maged continued, pacing back and forth, not able to control this fetish.

"The witness named Camillia Sobhy seems to be remembering names in a suspicious piecemeal fashion. What's the deal with her? And what about the drugs found in her bag, which she claims were planted there? Are there any other names we need to know about? She must be questioned repeatedly because every name she discloses is either turning up dead or missing. As for Farida, bring her in immediately, no matter what it takes," the minister said forcefully. "I will not have more dead people on my watch, nor will I allow this cartel to kill our youth and nationals with this deadly substance," the minister said, his face expressing both determination and signs of stress.

"Police officers are on it, sir. But I need to request the assistance of two or more Special Forces Units to help my task force. We are dealing with a very well-connected drug cartel. They are constantly one step ahead – almost as if they know what my next move will be," Maged said, continuing to pace the floor, deep in thought.

"What are you trying to say, Officer Maged?" one of the aides said, his tone suddenly becoming angry. "You think there could be an inside mole?" he said, his eyes growing larger with anticipation.

"That's one of the main reasons I have come here alone today. I am sorry to say that I suspect there could be an inside informant," Maged said, looking apologetic at the minister and his aides. "I will need all the officers on my task force to be reviewed by an internal affairs committee. I will also ask that a new covert task force be formed with officers from the national security sector and that you consider this case to be a covert intelligence operation," Maged concluded, almost out of breath.

Maged was assured by the minister that his requests would be studied and granted in due course, and that a number of highly skilled and professional undercover intelligence agents would immediately be assigned and dispatched to the case. Feeling that he had accomplished the most important mission of his career, Maged thanked the minister and his aides for their time and cooperation. He walked out of the building feeling like he was about to go to war with an invisible enemy of the state. He felt an intense sense of patriotism wash over him as he got into the police car and told the assistant officer to drive back to the *Zamalek* police station. Maged needed to find Farida El Leithy, no matter what the price.

Once he arrived at the police station, he wore his black bulletproof vest over his shirt, and loaded his handgun. He was going to take a squad of three policemen and arrest Farida himself at her place of residence. *It's two o'clock in the afternoon, and Farida would probably still be home*, Maged thought to himself, given that she didn't have a regular nine-to-five job. He checked the GPS on his phone and found that she lived about 30 minutes away from the police station. The traffic was heavy on this Monday afternoon, and the routes were congested. Maged told the deputy officer to drive as fast as he could.

He was racing against time.

He had to get to Farida before the cartel got to her first. If they got to her first, she may not live another day.

Chapter Twenty
'Finding Farida'

Farida got dressed in a black loose-fitting tracksuit and pulled back her reddish-brown hair into a ponytail. She quickly dabbed on some makeup and wore the black *niqab* face cover she had purchased last night to disguise herself, just as Marwan had asked her to do. She still wasn't sure why he wanted her to be disguised today, but she then realized that if the cartel ever found out she was emotionally involved with Marwan, they would both pay the ultimate price. Not only would they be immediately expelled from the operation, but they could both face an even more sinister fate.

She knew she was now ready to start something new and exciting in her life. *The problem with this job*, she thought to herself, *was that it came with an overdose of adrenaline and oxytocin. The more you stayed in the operation, the higher the doses of both you needed.* With those exciting thoughts in mind, Farida packed a small black backpack with pepper spray, toiletries, lipstick, deodorant, and a small bottle of water. Her mission today was to get to know Marwan and perhaps initiate a romantic relationship in the process.

She locked the windows, making sure that her kitchen countertop was clean before she headed out of her apartment. The weather was chilly today, just as it had been for the past two weeks. Farida had ordered an Uber on her phone app and was now notified that the car was waiting for her downstairs. She felt that she needed the warmth that a vehicle provided when the weather was chilly outside, even though the leather on this car's back seat was very cold to the touch, making her entire body shudder. The driver was a young man in his thirties who didn't ask any questions and just simply followed the GPS directions on his phone.

Farida had received a location on her phone earlier this morning, showing the exact spot where she would meet Marwan on the Suez Road. Farida never asked Marwan why he had chosen such a secluded remote location for them to meet, and then she vividly remembered how she felt extremely uncomfortable when she met the 'mysterious man' with a thick French accent at a similar location only two days earlier.

Marwan sent her a text message asking for her exact whereabouts, saying that he had already arrived 20 minutes ago. Farida was beginning to feel butterflies in her stomach as the excitement and anticipation began to take control of her body. She was feeling flushed, and her skin became rosier. She looked at her face in her round compact mirror and saw a hopeful excited woman staring back at her. She couldn't recall the last time she had felt so excited to meet a man. It wasn't that Marwan was the man of her dreams or that she found him overly attractive, but rather that she was beginning to feel the need for a man's protection in this lonely world.

The car had now reached the beginning of the Suez Road, and Farida could see a number of cars queuing up ahead. Her heart sank as she realized that this could be a police checkpoint. She felt scared and told the driver to turn the car around after suddenly deciding to abort the meeting with Marwan today. She felt very uneasy with the whole situation and wanted to go back home, deciding to call the whole thing off. She thought it would be safer if they met another time at a safer location.

The Uber driver did as he was told and made a U-turn to the left of the road. Farida texted Marwan, telling him that she was heading back home and that the whole thing wasn't making her feel comfortable. He responded immediately in an agitated and disappointed manner. She didn't understand why he was making such a fuss over this meeting today, suddenly feeling even more adamant to go back home.

The Uber driver received a text message on his phone, after which he took a detour from the main road and entered a narrower side street. Farida didn't think much of it, believing that perhaps he had found the main routes congested on his GPS map and opted for roads with less traffic. She was suffocating under the *niqab* face cover, so she slipped it off and stuffed it in her bag. After about 15 minutes, Farida realized that she didn't know where she was. The roads looked empty and almost deserted, so she asked the driver where they were. He looked at her in the rearview mirror and remained silent. She felt a knot brewing in her stomach.

"Where are we? I'm not familiar with these roads," Farida said, beginning to feel palpable fear creep into her heart, much like a slithering snake.

The driver didn't answer, continuing to drive on as if he had heard nothing. This made Farida even more fearful and somewhat angry. She didn't like his demeanor.

"Did you hear me? I want to know why you're taking these side streets? Why aren't you answering me? Look, I'm going to have to ask you to stop the car here now!" she said, using her most forceful, aggressive tone.

"Don't worry, madam, I was given instructions to take you to a specific location. You need not worry; just remain calm, and you'll be there very shortly," the driver said in a very monotone, calm voice.

Farida reached for her pepper spray and braced herself for what could potentially become a physical struggle in a moving vehicle. She texted Marwan to know what was happening, asking him how he would dare take her somewhere despite the fact that she had chosen to go back home. She received no answer from Marwan. She waited another five minutes, and still there was no response.

"Stop this car now, or else things will end very badly in here!" she screamed.

The driver slowed down and began to try to calm her down, but to no avail. He then stopped the car in the middle of the road and asked Farida to get out. He was fed up with her incessant threats and decided to punish her by leaving her alone in the cold weather on a deserted road. She immediately got out of the car and began walking away quickly, her eyes burning with tears. She didn't understand how Marwan could do such a bizarre thing to her.

She tried calling him again, and this time he picked up.

"You idiot, how dare you tell the Uber driver to take me somewhere when I told you I wanted to go back home?" she asked, shaking with both fear and anger.

"Farida, calm down. What are you talking about? I never did such a thing!" Marwan answered, not understanding what she was talking about.

"You liar! The Uber driver just told me that you wanted him to drive me to a specified location despite me telling him to take me back home!" she shouted, making a passerby turn around and stare at her.

"Farida, calm down. This is serious. I didn't receive any text from you today. My phone has been switched off since this morning because I was in a business meeting all day," Marwan said, his heart pounding as he could sense the fear in Farida's voice.

Farida stopped walking and sat down on the curb, trembling. She could sense that Marwan was telling her the truth, which made her even more fearful now.

"You sent me a text message this morning telling me to meet you at a specific location at three o'clock on the Suez Road! You also told me to wear a *niqab* in case I was being tailed by someone from the cartel!" Farida said, anxiously awaiting any confirmation from Marwan.

"Farida, that's not true! I never texted you this morning asking you to meet me, nor did I ask you to wear a *niqab*!" Marwan said, sensing that somebody was trying to frame him for something foul and to harm Farida as well.

Farida felt lost for words. It was beginning to rain, and she felt cold and alone on this deserted road in the middle of nowhere. A stray dog approached her, and she immediately stood up and began walking in the opposite direction. She needed to get out of this remote area before it got dark.

"Marwan, could you come get me from here, please?" she pleaded, feeling genuinely scared. "I will send you my location. Hurry because my battery is running out!" she added with a heightened sense of urgency.

Marwan agreed to pick her up and told her to try to remain in the same spot. He said he'd be there in about 30 minutes or less. Farida began pacing back and forth, all the while clutching her pepper spray in her right hand in case anyone appeared out of the blue and tried to harass her or physically assault her. It was in dangerous times like these that Farida thanked *Allah* that she had enrolled in self-defense classes two years ago. She began to perform breathing techniques, which she had learned from a YouTube tutorial, to try to calm herself down so that she wouldn't start hyperventilating. She knew her mild asthma was always exacerbated when she was either exercising or in a state of anxiety. She spotted a car approaching her from the right end of the road. The car flashed its headlights repeatedly, after which Farida let out a sigh of relief, thankful that Marwan had managed to make it so quickly, in spite of the rain, which was now falling harder than before.

She waved her hand to signal to him that she had seen him. The dark sedan slowed down and approached Farida, stopping two meters away from her. She walked over to the car and peered inside, but she couldn't see who was in the driver's seat because of the rain, which blurred her vision. Just as she was about to open the passenger door, one of the back seat doors opened, and she was pulled inside by a muscular man.

Farida was about to scream and fight the man until she looked at his face. She caught her breath.

"Farida, calm down. I am trying to save your life! You are now under arrest in connection with the Imperial Hotel murder case," Officer Maged said, feeling relieved that he had arrested Farida before she was abducted, or worse yet, killed, by the cartel.

She was now his only connection to the overseas cartel and perhaps his most valuable pawn in solving this case.

Chapter Twenty-One
'A Rock and a Hard Place'

Assem had the 'red dust' in his possession. His highly trained team on the ground at Port Said harbor had managed to smuggle the drug into Cairo undetected. He had successfully completed his end of the bargain and was now busy checking his bank account on the hour, hoping to find some movement on his balance, but nothing had been deposited yet. He cursed bitcoin out loud, but at the same time he understood the importance it played in covering up the dealings of the cartel's shady operations.

The officer was beginning to notice how Maged had been refraining from discussing anything of significance related to the case with him, which made him feel very uneasy. Assem's superiors were also totally relying on him to control the situation with Camillia, which he still hadn't executed to their satisfaction. He knew that offering her money would be a very dangerous strategy, so he believed that the next option would be for him to discuss with his superiors the option of eliminating her completely.

Assem initially intended to visit Camillia at her house and perhaps slip something toxic into her tea. But then he backtracked, concluding that this idea would be too naïve, and that it would most definitely backfire, making him a prime suspect in her death. He began constructing an alternate narrative. He wanted to try to convince Maged that she would be much more useful to the police if she was allowed to leave her house so that the perpetrators would try to contact her. In that case, the police could follow her and eventually track the killer. But what Assem's true desire was very different. He wanted Camillia to be easily marked and targeted by one of his hitmen.

Assem was suddenly jolted back to reality when he received an encrypted message from Marwan, who seemed to be in a state of complete disarray. Marwan told him about the debacle with Farida today and how she had been lured into a trap by an 'unknown entity.' He told him all about the remote location she had mentioned on the Suez Road and how she had claimed that he told her to disguise herself in a *niqab*.

Assem could immediately sense the presence of the cartel's modus operandi in this scenario, fearing that they were trying to perhaps eliminate her and, in the process, frame Marwan for her death. After all, both Marwan and Assem were well aware of how the cartel preferred conducting their business in remote locations along the Suez Road.

Assem now knew that the noose was tightening around his own neck and that the cartel had neither a heart nor a soul. The cartel's interest always reigned supreme. They were simply being used as pawns to cover up Mona's murder and to keep the lucrative 'red dust' dealings alive and well in Egypt. The fact that the cartel prohibited face-to-face meetings, except under very strict conditions and circumstances, made Assem even more certain that their strategy was always to 'divide and conquer.' The cartel knew that if members congregated regularly, they could attempt to expose the cartel or outright betray them.

There was nothing Assem could do now but try to placate Marwan until he found out exactly what was happening. He asked Marwan about Farida's current whereabouts and was told that her phone had been switched off for the past hour and that when he drove over to pick her up from the location she had sent him, she wasn't there. This was ominous news for Assem. As a seasoned police officer, he knew something wasn't right and that the onus was on him to find out what was really happening. It wasn't because he cared an iota about Farida's safety, but rather because he was now deeply concerned about his own.

Assem needed to find out what had happened to Farida without alerting the cartel in any way. If they found out that Marwan had even dared to have a direct relationship with Farida, they would all be severely punished. The only way for Assem to assess the situation was to contact

Farida directly, yet discreetly. He used his crypto-phone to send her a message and was surprised when she didn't respond. This was enough proof for him that she had either been abducted by the cartel or that she had possibly been arrested by Maged.

Both scenarios bode ill for him. He was now stuck between a rock and a hard place. He couldn't let the cartel find out that he knew something had happened to Farida, because that would confirm that the three of them were in contact without permission or directives to do so. Nor could he ask Maged directly if he had arrested Farida, because that would confirm that Assem was in direct contact with Marwan. The only solution, in his mind, was to go see Farida himself, under the pretense that he needed to question her again about the murder.

Assem couldn't sleep that night. He wanted to go visit Farida's residence first thing in the morning in order to find out exactly what had transpired the evening before. The pressure was building inside the *Zamalek* police station and in the entire police force to find Mona's killer. The pressure was simultaneously increasing for him to dispose of the 'red dust' that was now in his possession. He kept the capsules in over-the-counter bottles under his bathroom sink and had to wait to get clear instructions from the cartel on how to have them handed over to local dealers.

The next morning was day nine since the murder. Assem headed straight to the police station to try to see if Maged could give him any leads about Farida.

"Good morning, Maged," Assem said, holding a steaming glass cup of black tea. "Anything new in the case?" he asked, trying to read any odd facial expressions that may appear on Maged. He found none.

"Not really, except that I was thinking of removing Camillia's house arrest order and allowing her to move around freely. It might bring us one step closer to the killer," Maged said, looking at Assem's facial expressions in case he could read anything into them. He found nothing but a stone-cold face. Maged knew that Assem was just as well trained in police interrogation and in body language as he was himself, and he was now going to be extremely careful with every word he said to him and the rest of his team.

The Ministry of Interior had already begun running an internal affairs investigation into his task force, as per Maged's recommendation. Maged was almost certain that there was a mole that needed to be rooted out from inside his task force. He himself would have to undergo an internal investigation, as it was part of the department's routine procedure. He was well aware that when it came to Egypt's national security, nobody was above the law.

As distrust began to take hold of him, Maged didn't want Assem to find out that he had personally interrogated Farida for four continuous hours the night before and that all the acting in the world wouldn't have saved her when it came to Maged's interrogation tactics. He offered her a deal she couldn't afford to refuse. She had to come clean with everything she knew about the drug cartel and their means of operation in exchange for a lighter sentence for the role she had played in aiding and abetting the cartel's 'red dust' operations in Egypt.

Farida tried to deny she knew anything about the cartel at first, but when she was confronted with the evidence that the police had about her phony persona—the fact that her name was on 'the list' found in Suite 55 and that her cell phone was tapped—she began to seriously consider her options. What made Farida firmly decide to cooperate with the police was when Maged told her that one of the members of the operation, Murad Abdel Hamid, had been deliberately killed in a car crash and that another foreigner had gone missing. Farida immediately understood that the foreigner Maged was referring to was probably the 'mysterious man' with a thick foreign accent with whom she had met on the Suez road. Farida knew she now needed police protection to stay alive.

Realizing that Maged didn't know anything about Marwan, Farida decided to expose Marwan's involvement in the operation in exchange for an even lighter sentence. Maged felt that he had hit the jackpot when Farida testified that Marwan El-Meligy, the well-known shipping magnate, was involved in smuggling the 'red dust' into Egypt's harbors.

Maged now had a fourth name to add to his notepad, as he flipped it open and drew a thick red line with his marker, connecting Marwan's name to Farida and Mona.

But Farida decided she wasn't going to give everything she knew away so fast. While she did admit to having a facilitative role in the 'red dust' operation, she never mentioned Assem's name. She still wanted to remain somewhat loyal to the cartel, knowing that if she gave Assem's name away, they would surely find her and kill her, just as they did with the other two operators. She also knew that Assem was the pivotal link to all the ring members in Egypt. If he was exposed, the entire 'red dust' drug operation in Egypt would go bust.

Maged told her to go about her life as if nothing had happened, and to continue cooperating with the cartel, albeit under very strict police surveillance. He also told her that the cartel would definitely try to kill her, as she was now a liability to them, given that she had attempted to have direct contact with Marwan, blatantly going against their directives. She had also completed her part in the murder cover-up, and so she was now a sitting duck for them. He told Farida to continue getting closer to Marwan, finding out as much as she could about how the drugs were being smuggled into Egypt's ports.

The fact that she had been lured the day before into a potentially fatal trap left her with no choice but to walk a very thin line. The police and the cartel were heading into a deadly collision, and little did Officer Maged know that the snake was hatching in his very own nest.

Chapter Twenty-Two
'Kirmizi'

Assem ordered a deputy officer to bring Farida in for questioning. He didn't want to risk going to her residence knowing that her apartment was most likely being watched by the police, the drug cartel, or possibly both. He knew that he now had to be extremely vigilant in an increasingly complicated game of survival. He actually began thinking of how he himself would escape from Egypt if he ever felt that the noose had tightened too much around his neck. But when the deputy officer reached Farida's apartment, she was gone. Farida had actually gotten dressed in *niqab* attire, leaving her apartment an hour ago to meet Marwan at a secluded café on the Suez Road. She was wiretapped with a tiny earpiece in her left ear.

Maged, along with two national security agents, were already waiting inside a grocery van outside the café. They wore earpieces as they waited impatiently for Farida to arrive and to ask Marwan the questions Maged had told her to ask him the night before, when she was being interrogated. A security agent had already attached a GPS tracker to the OBDII port in Marwan's car, where it could directly receive power from the vehicle.

Farida's car arrived at exactly 10 o'clock. She parked her car and adjusted her earpiece, making sure it was in place under her *niqab*. She exited the car and found Marwan sitting at the very end of the café, on a table for four. She calmly walked to the table and sat down across from him, knowing that this was going to be her most important acting role ever, and she knew that she had to pull it off to perfection. She also knew the police were watching and listening to every word she was about to say.

"What is happening, Marwan? I waited for you to come pick me up from that deserted street last night, and you were late! I had to take a taxi," Farida said, faking a quiver in her voice.

"I came to you as fast as I could, and I panicked when I couldn't find you in the spot we had agreed on," Marwan said, feeling extremely awkward speaking to the woman he was attracted to as she sat in front of him in her black *niqab*.

"If it wasn't you who asked to meet me at that remote location, then it must be the cartel. They want me killed!" Farida said, choking back tears.

"But why would they want to kill you? You did as you were told. You simply told Officer Maged that you knew Mona and that she was your friend," he said, waving to the waiter to come get their order.

"Yes, but now I'm afraid to go back home. I feel that the cartel is watching me. They will kill me, Marwan! I will need to leave somewhere secure very soon," Farida said, lowering her voice, even though there weren't any other people sitting in the café.

"Look, I can find you a place to stay if you want," Marwan said, feeling more and more concerned about Farida's wellbeing.

"Don't you just wish we could leave the cartel and live a normal life, like everybody else? We already have enough money to leave," Farida said, in her sultry voice.

The waiter took down their orders for two cups of black tea and disappeared from sight.

"Not yet; there's a big shipment due to arrive in three days. It's for New Year's Eve. It will be the biggest and last one of the year, and I have to handle it. After that, I could think of leaving them for good," Marwan said, lowering his voice as much as he could.

"Did they even tell you where it's coming from? Or where this drug even originates from? They keep us in the dark, just using us as pawns, then discarding us like old dirty underwear," Farida said, faking anger in her voice.

"Look, all I know is that the container ship that's coming into the port here is called *Kirmizi*. It's coming from a port in Turkey. I don't want to say anymore. Why are you even asking me these questions? It doesn't concern you," Marwan said, feeling like he had already divulged too much information to her.

They both began sipping their steaming tea, with Farida having to clumsily lift her face veil to sip the hot drink.

"Kirmizi? That's a strange yet interesting name. Do you have any idea what it means?" Farida asked, feeling truly interested to know.

"It means 'red' in Turkish," he answered back, feeling increasingly agitated by her probing questions.

"Say no more. I understand. Listen, if you want to meet me again, I will always be dressed in a *niqab,* for safety," Farida said, as she picked up her bag and got ready to leave. She thanked Marwan for the cup of tea, which she left half full.

They agreed to meet again after three days. She told him she would send him an encrypted message that would self-destruct in two minutes. He had to answer it immediately within that time frame, or else she would consider the meeting 'aborted.'

Maged felt triumphant as he listened to this conversation play out, knowing that he had finally obtained several crucial and game changing pieces of information that would help him solve this complex case. He now knew where the 'red dust' originated from. More importantly, the police now knew the name of the container ship that was bringing in the lethal narcotic. He did not, however, know which Egyptian port was receiving the shipment. In his mind, that would have to be left to the intelligence officer to take care of.

The officer and the two agents smiled at one another as they removed their earpieces and headed back into the city. Maged had so much work ahead of him, but his mind kept working around his 'murder bytes.' He now knew for a fact that Turkey was the 'red dust's' point of origin, but he didn't believe that it was the point of manufacture. All that mattered to him now was the urgent need to intercept this shipment at any cost. Given that Marwan had just confessed that it was the last and biggest shipment of the year, Maged was certain that all the necessary manpower and logistics to seize the shipment would be made available to his newly created covert task force.

The two agents dropped Maged off at his home, where he immediately got into his car and headed to his appointment with Kamal Abdel Meguid, the experienced intelligence officer just assigned to the case by the National Security sector. He drove to the officer's home, located 20 minutes away from the Pyramids of Giza plateau, where he was greeted warmly and offered a cup of steaming Turkish coffee. The sun was about to set, giving Kamal's home a charming mystique.

Kamal was in his fifties, with medium height and build but with extraordinary intelligence and patriotism. His reputation was solid and exemplary, and Maged found him both pleasant and charismatic.

"Officer Kamal, thank you very much for agreeing to see me on such short notice," Maged said, as he sipped his thick coffee, enjoying the warmth of the sun on this cold Wednesday. They sat on Kamal's large terrace, where they could both speak in depth about the case and simultaneously enjoy the sun's last rays of the day.

"Officer Maged, this is my duty, and I was never one to turn my back on any case that may harm this country," Kamal said, looking into the distance and squinting his eyes. He adjusted his glasses and lit a cigarette, slowly inhaling, then puffing out the smoke sideways into the air.

"I need your experienced, fresh eyes to help us close in on this case. I'm sure you've been briefed about everything concerning the murder, and you can see the clear fingerprints of this drug cartel smeared all over it," Maged said rhetorically, hoping the officer would stub out his cigarette and give him his undivided attention.

"I was indeed thoroughly briefed. I even know that you already have two of the local cartel members under strict surveillance," Kamal said, stubbing out his cigarette as if he could hear Maged's thoughts. "How do you think I can be of most help to you in this covert task force?" Kamal asked with a genuine tone of patriotism.

"Given your experience with drug cartels and organized crime overseas, what do you know about the drug route from Turkey to Egypt?

Do you have any idea where this new drug, 'red dust,' originates from and how it gets into the country?" Maged asked, putting down his small cup of coffee and looking intently at Kamal's face.

"Look, Turkey probably isn't the manufacturing point for the 'red dust.' It is a country mostly used as a land bridge between Afghanistan and the West through the Balkans. You may call it 'the Balkan route,' if you like," Kamal said, having studied this specific drug route for many years. "But the route from Afghanistan may not be the same for 'red dust.' From what I understand, 'red dust' is new, odorless, and lethal because it is used as a base. This makes it almost impossible for sniffer dogs to recognize," Kamal said, folding his arms across his chest and looking into the distance towards the pyramids.

"So where do you think it's manufactured? We need to cut off the tentacles of this dangerous cartel. I cannot trace the route of the drug if I don't have the point of origin and the route to Egypt," Maged said, feeling hungry for more information.

"I believe this drug is being manufactured somewhere remote in Eastern Europe, then smuggled through the Balkan route to Turkey. From Turkey, it is then smuggled here via maritime routes. It is easy to track the maritime shipping routes from Turkish ports to Egyptian ports. Leave that to me, Officer Maged," Kamal said, as he lit another cigarette.

"Welcome to our new covert task force. I will need to focus on Farida and Marwan. I also have Camillia to worry about. I think it's time for me to pay her a visit and then perhaps set her free under strict surveillance," Maged said, as if speaking to himself. "I need to begin using her as bait to lure the cartel in," Maged added.

"Maged, as I just told you, I know where I can help. But we will also need the assistance of an intelligence agent to explain the structure of drug cartels overseas and how they operate. If we really want to cut off the tentacles of this powerful cartel, then we must understand their organizational hierarchy. Only then can we uncover the identity of the drug lord responsible and bring the entire cartel down," Kamal explained, impressing Maged with his strategic mindset.

"Who do you propose would be the most knowledgeable and experienced agent in that arena?" Maged asked, looking at the swirling cigarette smoke being exhaled around him.

"I suggest we bring in agent Rawan. She's incredibly smart and impressively tech-savvy. She will help us disrupt their communication networks as well as trace their financial routes to local cartel operators here. Your role, Officer Maged, is to find out from Farida how local operators are getting paid for their work," Kamal said, adding new dimensions of inquiry into the case.

Maged left Kamal's house armed with a plan of action, a strategic roadmap. He felt that Officer Kamal would be extremely beneficial to the case, and he was thankful that the Minister of Interior had agreed to form the covert task force, incorporating top-tier agents of the highest caliber. The newly formed covert task force was dubbed, 'Code Red.'

Maged drove back home, after which he fell into a deep sleep. He hadn't slept so deeply since the murder had occurred 11 days ago. He knew he needed every ounce of energy to boost his mental strength. He was about to face a herculean task. It was now a covert war for the country. He was determined that it would only be a matter of time before the 'red dust' drug route was obliterated from existence.

And time was ticking.

Chapter Twenty-Three
'Agent Rawan'

Camillia sat next to her mother, watching her eat white rice and a piece of leftover boiled chicken. She felt sorry for her, as she was now chewing her food with difficulty, given that she had lost so many of her teeth during the past few years. Camillia yearned to be set free to walk the streets again and to be able to mingle with people. She missed getting up every morning and heading to work, even though she knew it wasn't the most glorious job in the world, but it gave her something to look forward to every day.

She hadn't heard from Officer Maged or Assem in the past three days and was beginning to wonder if this was going to become her new way of life. She got up with a heavy heart and began dusting the small flat when she suddenly heard the now familiar three knocks on the front door. She excitedly pulled her headscarf over her silky hair and went to see who it was.

"Officer Maged, good afternoon!" Camillia said, hoping he was here to set her free once and for all.

"Camillia, we need to talk," the officer said, sitting down on the old gray sofa near the door. "I need to know the remaining two names on 'the list.' You said there were five names and that you could only remember three so far. You need to jog your memory a little bit more! Now!" he almost shouted, knowing that the last two names were probably all he needed to bring the killer and the entire cartel to justice.

"As I told you, officer, I'm having trouble remembering the last two names! But I'll keep trying to remember, even though it's been 12 days now since the murder," Camillia said, trying to sound as convincing as possible. She was planning on revealing one more name to Officer Maged, provided he agreed to set her free. She was patiently waiting to hear anything from him that would secure her freedom and offer her police protection.

"Let me tell you one of the names this time! Does the name Marwan El Meligy ring a bell, Camillia?" Maged asked forcefully, knowing that he had definitely struck a chord when her face turned pale and her eyes widened.

"Marwan? El-Meligy? Maybe; I'm not sure. It sounds a bit familiar. I don't know; I can't be sure, Maged *beh*," Camillia answered, her heart pounding out of her chest and her mouth becoming dry.

She looked away, knowing that she had fallen into a trap of her own making, the police now being one step ahead of her. She kept thinking of how she could have possibly been so naïve to attempt to play a mental game with the police.

Maged watched her facial expressions turn from initial excitement when he entered the small apartment to palpable fear when he mentioned Marwan's name. He was now certain that she knew more than she was telling him and that she was bound to end up in prison for obstruction of justice and withholding information. He told her he would consider putting her in jail if she didn't come clean about the other two names.

"Officer Maged, it's been 12 days since the murder; do you really think it's that easy for me to remember names that I casually read from a piece of paper?" Camillia said, trying to defend herself.

Maged was about to respond when he received a text message on his cellphone. It was officer Kamal telling him that he had set up a meeting with intelligence agent Rawan at three o'clock that evening at his home. Maged was now confident that with every passing hour he was making headway toward finding the killer and eventually obliterating this nefarious cartel from existence.

He turned his attention to Camillia once again.

"Look Camillia. You will never be set free until you remember the last two names on that list. I already know that you know the last name on the list. I will give you 48 hours to remember. Try as hard as you can to brainstorm within that frame of time because after that you won't like the consequences," Maged said, as he turned his back and made his way to the old wooden door.

Maged left Camillia's house and drove directly to officer Kamal's house. He knew Camillia would contact him very soon to confirm Marwan El Meligy's name. But now he badly needed to know the final name on the list.

He followed the route on his cellphone's GPS and found that he had about an hour of driving from *Boulaq* to get to the Pyramids area. His mind was racing as he felt a rush of adrenaline wash over him. The thought of meeting agent Rawan was giving him the positive feeling that she was going to be an important component in this top-caliber covert task force. They needed to find out how the cartel paid their local operators in Egypt. That was going to be vital information that they would hand over to Interpol. Rawan would be able to intercept and disrupt their chain of communication, wreaking havoc and destabilizing the cartel's transfer of money in the region.

He found a parking spot under Kamal's building. He was dressed in a pair of gray pants, a white shirt, and a black wool sweater, his sunglasses resting on his dark brown hair. He wanted this meeting to be professional but with a casual air. The three of them were going to form a covert task force that was about to unleash a massive assault on this cartel. There was no room for error here, only space for dedication, resilience, and meticulousness.

"Officer Maged, please come in," Kamal said, showing Maged to the outdoor terrace where they had met the day before.

"Thank you, officer Kamal; I am looking forward to meeting agent Rawan; you spoke very highly of her," Maged said, taking the same seat he had occupied the previous day.

"She will be here in exactly five minutes. She has already been briefed on the information regarding the case, and she's more than ready to commence her role," Kamal said, lighting a cigarette and inhaling deeply.

The doorbell rang. Kamal stubbed out his cigarette and went to open the door quickly. Rawan walked onto the terrace, surprising Maged by how young and foreign-looking she appeared. She was slim, dressed in black pants and a heavy green jacket, with her light curly brown hair tied up in a messy bun.

"Officer Maged, I'm agent Rawan, here to be of service to the 'Code Red' task force," she said, sounding very confident and business-like. She sat down and flipped open her laptop case, sliding her state-of-the-art Lenovo onto the table.

"Agent Rawan, I am pleased to have you on board our team. Officer Kamal tells me you have been briefed and that you're ready to explain how you can disrupt this cartel's means of communication and online monetary transfer chains," Maged said, wanting to get down to business as soon as possible.

"Before I explain what I intend to do, I want to say that I have already begun my investigations, using my informants to find out how this particular cartel is structured. I can tell you that this cartel is relatively new, just like the drug they are smuggling into Egypt and into other countries in Europe," she said, turning the laptop around so that the screen faced them.

"Do you have any idea who the drug lord is? His code names? Where does he reside? Any information at all?" Maged asked, wanting all the information he could get his hands on so that they could pass it on to Interpol.

"I'm working on all that. But I can tell you that they use very highly sophisticated Sky ECC crypto-phones, which are a very common communication tool for organized crime. These phones can transmit self-destructing messages as well as secure audio messages. Users can even wipe off the contents of the phone using what is known as a 'panic password.' Of course, this is all paid for using bitcoin," she said, pulling out a bottle of water from her bag. "I will of course explain in detail how they use bitcoin to transfer money, but at a later point," she added with confidence.

"What can you tell us now that could bring us one step closer to catching the killer?" Maged asked, wanting some information that he could work on immediately.

"I can tell you that this cartel is using 'falcons' in Egypt to watch police movements. These operators are dubbed 'falcons,' as they are the eyes and ears of the cartel on the streets here. They are also using hitmen to assassinate members of the cartel here who don't abide by their rules or ones they no longer have any use for. One of these hitmen was probably contracted to kill the co-pilot, Murad Abdel Hamid, in a staged car accident, and possibly also Demir Dogan, who has been missing for a week now," Rawan said, glancing at her laptop every now and then and adjusting her eye glasses on the bridge of her nose.

"This all makes sense to me, agent Rawan. That is usually how cartels are structured. But what do you know about the upper two tiers of their organizational structure? We need to know who's their lieutenant in Egypt, and of course who's their drug lord abroad," Kamal interjected, lighting a cigarette, and then looking far off toward the Pyramids plateau.

"I am working on gathering that information as we speak. But what I will need from you, officer Kamal, is intelligence on their drug route and point of origin. 'Code Red' task force will have to work closely together on all fronts so that we could close in on them. We also have to work very closely with Interpol," Rawan said, looking directly at officer Kamal, who seemed to enjoy exhaling his cigarette smoke in swirls, high up in the air.

"I was at Camillia's house before coming here, and I can assure you that she will come clean with the remaining two names. I confronted her about Marwan El Meligy's name, and I could tell that she's familiar with his name. All I need from her now is the final name on 'the list,' and I am sure she will disclose it to me to reduce her prison sentence. She's obstructing the procedure on the case and withholding crucial information," Maged said, watching Kamal's stone-cold expression as he gazed off into the misty distance.

"What about Marwan? He will be very important for us to trace the route of the final big shipment coming in for New Year's in a week," Kamal said, as he stubbed out his second cigarette and lit his third.

"Marwan is being watched around the clock now, and of course Farida is working closely with us now to reduce her prison sentence. I will question Farida in depth about how she gets paid for her role in their operations," Maged said, looking at Rawan and Kamal. "That would help you, agent Rawan, to track the bitcoin route to her account," Maged added, giving her a nod.

They ended their meeting and agreed to meet again in 48 hours, giving each other only two days to come up with the new information. It was a race against time for the three of them. But before leaving Kamal's house, they decided to bring in a crucial fourth 'Red Code' member. Officer Kamal was going to bring in Navy Admiral Mostafa Soweilam on board. They needed the expertise and knowledge of someone who knew the maritime sailing routes from Turkey and Europe to Egypt like the back of their own hand. Admiral Mostafa was one of the top navy admirals who knew and sailed these waters better than any other.

Their next meeting was going to be held in a classified location, one that was equipped with one of the most technologically advanced communication systems and satellite imagery in the world. Maged wasn't familiar with this location, but it was obvious to him that both officer Kamal and agent Rawan were very keen on holding their next meeting there. They referred to this location as the 'Bunker,' and they were going to give Maged the exact time and location only one hour ahead of the meeting. Their meetings were going to be strictly confidential; nobody other than the four of them would be privy to anything that was discussed inside this communication bunker.

Maged drove back home with much on his mind. He made himself a cheese sandwich and began pacing back and forth, clicking his ballpoint pen furiously as his mind worked the 'murder bytes' in overdrive. He opened his notepad and pulled out his thick red marker, drawing a pyramid structure composed of four tiers. He filled in the bottom tier with the word 'falcons' and the third tier with the word 'hitmen.' He then wrote the word 'lieutenant' in huge letters in the second tier. It was going to be his job to find out who the cartel's lieutenant was in Egypt, in a frantic race against time. Kamal and Rawan would work together to identify the drug lord abroad, working very closely with Interpol. They had only 48 hours to come up with the required information before their next meeting, and the shipment was due to arrive in seven days.

The 'Code Red' task force was adamant about celebrating the destruction of the 'red dust' cartel on New Year's Eve.

Chapter Twenty-Four
'Extraction'

Farida woke up with a heavy feeling in her heart. The skies were cloudy, and there was a chilly breeze in the air. She was under immense pressure to find out from Marwan when the big shipment was coming to Egypt, as well as its point of origin. She was going to meet him at a café in two hours, where she would be wiretapped under her *niqab* with an earpiece in her left ear. She had to extract this information from him to reduce her prison sentence, and she was willing to do whatever it took to get that information. She knew she had to be very careful not to appear too pushy; after all, the last thing she wanted was for Marwan to suspect that she was meeting him for her own benefit.

She sent Marwan an encrypted message, asking him to meet her at the public promenade in *Zamalek*, overlooking the Nile. She explained to him that they didn't need to meet on the Suez Road again, as she was already concealing her identity by dressing in a *niqab*. But in reality, Maged had told her to ask to change the meeting venue because he needed to be near the Zamalek police station. He had a very important meeting today with the internal affairs committee, and they were going to brief him about their findings.

Farida purposely drowned herself in her favorite perfume, making sure her nails were manicured, coated with her trademark red nail polish, even though she was going to slip on black gloves. She had to pretend that she was falling in love with Marwan, all the while trying to subtly seduce him into telling her all that she wanted to know. She found it so ironic that at one point in her life she desperately wanted to become an actress, when now she felt tremendous anxiety to play the biggest and most important role of her life.

Maged sat in a dark Chrysler van with two officers at a vantage point where he could watch Farida disembark from the Uber. His adrenaline was pumping today, looking at his watch every few minutes. They were all fitted with ear pieces and the van had two computer screens rolling live audio transmission. Maged clenched his fist, knowing he had no time to lose and that both Rawan and Kamal were working against the clock to uncover their assigned information before their next meeting.

Farida arrived in an Uber and immediately walked toward the promenade entrance, where an undercover police officer was already waiting, watching her from a nearby bench. Marwan was waiting for her near the entrance, smiling at her as she walked toward him. She still could not get used to walking in her new attire, feeling like she was about to trip over with every brisk step.

"Marwan, thank you for coming here today. I know you hate being in public, but don't worry; nobody will suspect anything here. The promenade is actually crowded today, and we are even less noticeable here than in a café somewhere," Farida said, her eyes searching around for any onlookers.

She was afraid she was being tailed by the cartel, but was repeatedly reassured by Maged that his police team was closely monitoring her every move.

"Farida, I don't think we should meet in person again. I really want to get to know you better, but I'm afraid for both of us. The cartel is definitely watching us, and we could get ourselves in very serious trouble," Marwan said, looking at every passerby with suspicion from behind his dark sunglasses.

"I understand, but I really wanted to speak to you because I'm scared. We're both scared. That's why I'm coming to ask you if you would ever consider leaving the cartel after this last big shipment comes in from Turkey. We can both make enough money to elope somewhere and live normal lives," Farida said, looking at Marwan with teary eyes.

"That's a possibility, but it has to be done with immaculate precision," he responded, feeling his emotions begin to surge for this woman, her fragrance stirring up his senses.

"Why don't we elope from the port of entry of this shipment? You could manage it with your men on the ground, and then we could escape on one of the container ships to any other country. You'll get your payment through bitcoin, and hopefully the police won't be able to trace its origin," she said, in her most sultry voice.

"That could be a doable scenario, but it's not that easy. Don't forget that Assem is watching my every move. He's definitely watching you too," Marwan said, giving away Farida's most prized secret.

Farida's heart sank when Assem's name was mentioned, knowing that she had now lost Maged's trust forever. Her earpiece suddenly felt like molten lava as she realized that she now had nobody's protection, but Maged's. Assem's head was now probably more valuable to Maged than anybody else's.

Maged's face turned pale, then it turned into a bright crimson hue when he heard Assem's name being mentioned. His heart began to beat with such vigor that the two officers with him had to pat him on the shoulder to calm him down. He couldn't believe that his long-time police partner was involved with this nefarious drug cartel. Maged was very suspicious there was a mole inside his task force, but he never thought, even for a second, that it could actually turn out to be Assem. Maged wanted to seize this opportune moment to collect recorded audio evidence against Assem, evidence that could be damning against him with the internal affairs committee. He quickly began directing Farida to ask Marwan specific questions through her earpiece.

"Ask him to tell you how Assem is involved with this big shipment," Maged directed her through his tiny microphone.

"Marwan, do you think Assem would ever join us, or do you think he would betray us for them?" Farida asked, knowing that she had to extract the answers to Maged's questions quickly.

"Assem is on his own side, Farida. Don't you dare utter a word to him about what we're discussing or where our plans might lead us. He only has his own interest at heart. I've met with him in person, and I know how shrewd, cunning, and ruthless he is," Marwan answered, as he watched the people around him.

"Yes, I don't trust Assem either. He scares me too, somehow. I also know he's watching me, and that's why I change into a *niqab* before I meet you. Maybe you could convince him to help smuggle in this last big shipment to local dealers, then he could quit and escape abroad somewhere," she said, trying to sound like the damsel in distress.

"Never! My only contact with Assem is when my superiors direct me to deliver or receive sensitive information from him."

"Farida, you seem to have forgotten that as operators we shouldn't be in contact with one another at all," Marwan said, shifting from on foot to the other, feeling a sudden urge to leave.

Maged then told her to abort the meeting and ask Marwan to meet her tomorrow in a more crowded location. She did as she was told, and Marwan agreed to meet her the next day near *Al-Hussein* mosque, at four o'clock in the afternoon. With that being confirmed, Marwan and Farida went their separate ways. Maged now had all the audio evidence he needed to directly implicate Assem in the 'red dust' cartel. He told the two agents with him to take him directly to the *Zamalek* police station, where the internal affairs committee was waiting for him to arrive.

The officer walked briskly into his office, finding two officers dressed in civilian suits seated at his desk across from one another. They looked up at him as he walked in and quickly asked him to shut the door. He did as he was told and couldn't wait to know what they were going to tell him about their investigation.

"Officer Maged, our internal affairs committee has some interesting findings to share with you. Our investigation has revealed that Officer Assem may be implicated in this murder case by submitting falsified evidence and using unlawful tactics to intimidate witnesses," one of them said, without divulging any further details.

"He's done much more than that! I now have crucial audio recordings, which I just gathered just before coming here, that I need to add to your investigation. I have recorded two operators discussing his role in the cartel's operation in Egypt!" Marwan said, eager to have his partner severely punished in a court of law for aiding, abetting, obstructing the law, withholding information, and benefiting from a nefarious overseas criminal organization.

"Our team will review your audio recordings and submit them as material evidence in our investigation against him. Please take great care when dealing with him from now on. He's now under very strict surveillance," the other man said, as they both got up to leave Maged's office.

Maged felt vindicated after this meeting. But he also knew that Assem was a very well trained police officer and that catching him red-handed would be no easy feat. It was now clear to Maged that Assem had taken advantage of his connections as a police officer to smuggle the 'red dust' from the port into Cairo, after Marwan's cargo handlers ensured that it was securely offloaded from the container ship. Maged began pacing back and forth, trying to control the overwhelming sense of betrayal that he now felt toward Assem.

Maged wanted to alert Rawan and Kamal about this sudden new development in the case, knowing quite well that the 'Code Red' task force was well on its way to a full faceoff with the cartel. Even though his 'murder bytes' were now falling quickly into place, his mind kept reverting to Camillia's list of names. He now wondered if Assem's name was the last one on that list. And if it was, he was now furious that Camillia had withheld such damning evidence from the police. But for now, Maged wanted to leave the police station quickly, not wanting to bump into Assem by chance and to have to mask his feelings of utter disgust and sheer anger. He was about to exit his office when a white rectangular envelope on his desk caught his attention. It was stamped by the coroner's office. He tore open the envelope and found the autopsy report he had requested on the death of Murad Abdel Hamid.

The toxicology report showed no traces of illegal substances in the co-pilot's system, nor did his body show any evidence of forced trauma. It appeared as though the co-pilot had died in a fatal car crash, but Maged thought otherwise. He was certain that one of the cartel's hitmen had finished Murad off for some reason. The cartel was adept at covering its footsteps, but Maged knew they were far from being perfect, having left evidence behind in Suite 55. That evidence was currently being investigated by the most qualified forensics team in the country.

The gray hairs and the off-white button that Camillia had reported seeing in one of the sinks in the suite on the morning of the murder were actually found and bagged that morning by the forensics team. That team was now working frantically on those crucial pieces of evidence, trying to extract DNA from the few strands of hair to match them against the list of suspects which Maged had submitted to the Ministry of Interior earlier this morning.

Maged knew it was only a matter of time before the killer was found and brought to justice, but it had to be done with supreme confidentiality and professionalism. Even if the police were already closing in on the killer's identity, Maged found it prudent at this time to keep that information under wraps until the green light was given to make the arrest. Maged wanted the killer to be arrested in tandem with the complete and unequivocal demolition of the entire 'red rug' cartel. He didn't want the 'falcons' and the hitmen to hide in the shadows. He wanted them to continue operating so that the dragnet could root them out, one by one.

The 'Code Red' task force was going to manage the entire dragnet operation, wanting to not only capture the killer but, more importantly, obliterate the cartel from the face of the earth.

Chapter Twenty-Five
'Day 13'

Assem woke up this morning with a very unsettled feeling, having heard from his colleagues the night before that two officers from the Internal Affairs department had visited Maged at the *Zamalek* police station. Coupled with the fact that Maged had been avoiding him for the past few days under the pretense that he was too busy to have a one-on-one briefing, made Assem suspect that something was going on. It was rare for Assem to get this sense of dread in the pit of his stomach. As a well-trained police officer, he always trusted his gut instinct.

He had the unfamiliar urge to begin distributing the 'red dust' capsules as soon as possible. He knew that the quicker he could dispose of those capsules, the quicker he could start planning his own escape from the country. He had the feeling that he was intentionally being left out of Maged's police briefings and that Marwan and Farida were involved in some kind of emotional entanglement. His superiors were also pressuring him to distribute the capsules to his local drug dealer's network as soon as possible, all of which made him begin to suspect that a clandestine operation was being mounted by both sides and that he was being given the cold shoulder treatment by both parties.

Assem instinctively began sending text messages to his 'falcons' on the ground, inquiring if they were sensing anything unusual happening. One of them responded that Farida had gone out of her flat twice during the past week and that Marwan had also left his apartment twice during the same time frame, besides taking his usual office route on workdays. Assem didn't need any further confirmation that Marwan and Farida were having social meetings and that they could very well be conspiring against the cartel, or worse yet, against him.

He asked his 'falcons' to keep a very close eye on both Marwan and Farida and to report back to him immediately if there were any updates. But this time he directed them to have Marwan and Farida tailed whenever they went out. He had to obtain visual footage that he could then pass on to his superiors that Marwan and Farida were meeting without being directed to do so by the cartel. Assem knew he had to save his own skin for as long as he could. He was also very well aware of how Murad Abdel Hamid had been killed in an apparent car crash and that Demir Dogan had never been found, despite Interpol's rigorous efforts to arrest him.

Assem surmised that the cartel was using its hitmen to kill off unwanted operators and that Marwan and Farida could possibly be next in line, given that they were not adhering to the cartel's strict rules of engagement. He was also certain that even though he held the title of 'lieutenant' in Egypt's 'red dust' chain of command, he still wasn't immune to being killed off by one of the cartel's assassins. All these scenarios kept playing out in his mind, making him more eager to dispose of the capsules that were stashed in a plastic bag under his sink.

He was going to have to meet with each drug dealer in a different location to make sure that he wasn't being tailed by anyone. He had three bottles of 'red dust,' each bottle containing a hundred capsules of the potent, odorless powder base. The cartel always sent him encrypted messages with the exact time and location for each drop-off, but now he couldn't wait any longer to receive the information. It had been five days since he had received the 'red dust' from Marwan's port handlers in Port Said, and now he was itching to get rid of the bottles as soon as possible.

Assem had no idea that his apartment was now being watched by three intelligence agents sitting in a dark van which was fitted with two audio and visual monitors. His flat had been bugged the day before, and the intelligence agents were now listening to and watching his every move. His car was also being tracked by a GPS tracker, which was secretly planted at dawn underneath his car. The two officers from the Internal

Affairs Department wasted no time acting quickly on the sensitive and dangerous audio information which Maged had provided. The wiretap on Farida had proven extremely beneficial in implicating Marwan and Assem in the cartel's local drug dealing operations in Egypt.

Oblivious to the fact that he was now under surveillance, Assem nervously tapped his fingers on his dining table, becoming extremely impatient, wondering why the cartel would wait for five whole days without sending him clear instructions on how and when they wanted the 'red dust' handed over to local distributors. He felt so uneasy that he thought of sending his superiors an encrypted message from his Skyphone inquiring about the locations and dates for the drop-off. He decided to go ahead and send the message, but he received no immediate answer, which was highly unusual given his 'lieutenant' ranking in the cartel's organizational hierarchy.

As Assem continued to conjure up dark scenarios in his mind, Maged was receiving constant live updates from the intelligence agents who were watching and listening to the audio and visual feed coming from Assem's apartment. Feeling secure that Assem's movements were being closely monitored, Maged instructed Farida to find out from Marwan which port would be the point of sailing and which was the destination port. He told her she had to meet with Marwan that very evening because he needed that sensitive information immediately. He was about to have the most important meeting of his life tomorrow with agent Rawan and officer Kamal in the so-called 'bunker,' Time was running out, and he had to come up with the required information by tomorrow morning's meeting.

Farida did as she was told and immediately sent Marwan a message asking him to meet her at the crowded *Khan El Khalili* open-air bazaar in downtown Cairo. She told him she would don her *niqab* as usual and that they would be able to sit at a restaurant in the bustling tourist market, secretly planning an escape after Marwan completed the upcoming shipment. Marwan was excited to meet Farida, even though he wasn't delighted with the fact that she was covered from head to toe in a long garb, and that her face was concealed too. But he was ready to do anything at this point to get closer to Farida, feeling an increasing attraction to her, even though he was well aware that this palpable attraction could cost them both their lives.

They met at four o'clock in the afternoon at a kebab restaurant overlooking *Al-Hussein* mosque. Farida was getting accustomed to the discomfort of walking in her long attire and was becoming more comfortable covering her face from the world. She actually felt relieved that she didn't need to wear makeup anymore and that dyeing her hair was no longer irking her.

Having her identity concealed was actually giving her a newfound sense of freedom, making her mind focus on what needed to be done and the arduous task ahead of her. She knew she had to make Marwan answer all her questions and that those answers would give her leverage with the police to be more lenient regarding her prison sentence.

She walked toward the restaurant, trying not to trip over her long garb, bumping occasionally into pedestrians as she made her way through the congested market. She kept glancing around, wondering where Officer Maged had chosen to position himself to listen, and perhaps even watch, the meeting she was about to have with Marwan. She felt thankful that her *niqab* was making her feel warm on this chilly afternoon in December and that her black gloves were engulfing her with a sense of tingling warmth. She sat down at a table for two and waited for Marwan to show up. She remembered that he usually made it to their meetings before she did, as she nervously glanced at her watch, hoping he would miraculously appear amidst the crowds.

"Farida!" she heard Marwan say from behind her as he took the seat across the small table from her. He wore dark sunglasses, a cap, and a black training suit in an obvious effort to conceal his own identity too.

"Marwan, I'm happy to see you again," Farida said, knowing that this could very well be their last meeting.

"We have to make it brief. I hate being in public, as you well know. Is there anything urgent you need? Are you alright?" Marwan asked, his voice sounding a little less warm than she had expected.

"You sound irritated. Is something wrong? I completely understand that you're anxious about the upcoming shipment. But don't worry, you've handled several before," she said.

"This one is different. It's truly huge, and the danger is equally huge. The sailing route has been changed all of a sudden," Marwan said, sounding distraught.

"Where was it coming from initially?" Farida asked, seizing the opportunity to give the police crucial information.

"From Turkey, as you already know. I shouldn't be telling you this, but I feel we're in this together now. It was supposed to come from Mersin Port in southern Turkey, but now that route will be changed. The destination port is probably going to be changed as well," Marwan said, his eyes looking around nervously.

"But you need to know the new destination in order to prepare your people. Besides, your men were probably already so acquainted with the previous port destination," Farida said, trying to indirectly make Marwan tell her more about where the upcoming shipment was sailing to.

"Definitely," Marwan whispered. "They knew the harbor of Port Said like the back of their hands. I had my contacts there, and they always had my back. Now I don't know if they will be able to manage this huge shipment from an unfamiliar port," he said, oblivious to the fact that he was giving away damning incriminating information against himself.

They sipped their hot black tea and continued talking for another ten minutes, after which Marwan told Farida he needed to get back to his office to finish some important paperwork. He promised to meet her again in the next couple days, after which they both left the crowded bazaar, walking away with much on their minds.

Maged listened to this conversation with much weighing on his own mind. While he had just found out that the usual maritime route was from Mersin Port in Turkey to Port Said harbor, he was now faced with the dilemma of discovering the new route for the big shipment. He needed Farida to keep probing Marwan for answers. But Maged felt that something in Marwan's voice and demeanor seemed to be different this time. He began to worry that Marwan was having suspicions about Farida or that the cartel was trying to intentionally mislead Marwan into thinking that there would be a new shipping route for the final shipment of the year. He also began to wonder whether the cartel was misleading Marwan on purpose because they suspected that he was being watched and that Farida could be wiretapped. Maged knew that nobody would be that cunning and shrewd, except for Assem.

Maged wondered if Assem knew he was being watched and that his apartment had been bugged. For someone as well trained as himself, Maged was now certain that he was coming head to head with his mirror self. They both knew each other's minds too well. They both knew how the other's mind operated. But Maged had to keep up the charade, acting as though he knew nothing about his partner's involvement with the cartel. He had to pretend that he still trusted the very man who was now his nemesis.

One thing Maged was absolutely sure of now was that this was going to be a face-off of epic proportions.

Chapter Twenty-Six
'The Last Name'

Maged had only a few hours left to find out what the point of origin of the shipment was as well as its destination before his meeting with Rawan and Kamal tomorrow morning. He kept pacing back and forth in his apartment, clicking his blue ballpoint pen until his fingers became red and sore. His mind was racing against time, against Assem, and against the cartel. He didn't want to arrest Assem just yet, wanting him to be the bait with which the 'Code Red' task force would bring down the entire drug cartel. He knew that arresting both Assem and Marwan now would only serve to push the cartel into hiding, but he wanted it to implode from the inside out.

With only a few hours left before nightfall, Maged decided to pay Camillia a visit. Her 48-hour window frame was now over. He desperately needed to know the last name on 'the list.' He had to make sure that it was Assem's name and not somebody else's that the police weren't aware of yet in their investigation. But this time, he was going to have to use the 'bad cop' tactic with Camillia. He needed to show her that she would pay dearly for not coming forth earlier with the information she knew and that if she didn't reveal the last name on 'the list,' she would be strapped with a very heavy prison sentence.

He parked his car under Camillia's building, looking left and right until he spotted the policeman who was keeping watch on her building. He gave the policeman a courteous nod and ascended the stairs to Camilllia's apartment. He knocked three times, as usual, on the old wooden door. Camillia opened the door immediately, pulling her head scarf around her face as she let him in.

"Camillia, how's your mother's health? I hope she's receiving her medicine regularly," Maged asked, sitting on the now familiar old gray sofa near the door.

"She's alright Maged *beh,* thank you for asking. Am I going to be set free now?" Camillia asked, feeling excited to be speaking to someone other than her mother.

"Camillia, we had a deal. I'm here to tell you that your time is up. You have to tell me the last name on 'the list.' I don't know why you've kept these names a secret from the police! What did you think you were going to gain? Did you think you could extort money from the killer? Do you have any idea what your prison sentence will be for obstructing justice and withholding information from the police in a murder investigation?" Maged said, pacing back and forth, trying to control his fury.

"I never withheld information from the police. I'm telling you the names as I remember them," Camillia said, hoping the quiver in her voice wouldn't give her away.

"You really think I believe you? You really think I believe you're remembering names that you briefly looked at two weeks ago? I know you have that list. You must give it to me right now because it may have the killer's fingerprints all over it!" Maged said, trying to be forceful in his tone.

"But if I have it, it will also have my fingerprints on it!" Camillia said, realizing that if she gave the paper to Maged, the judge may rule that she was either an accomplice or the killer.

"Give me the paper, Camillia! I will make sure that the judge understands that you were afraid because you were threatened and that the 'red dust' capsules that were found in your bag were planted there to keep you quiet," Maged said, hoping she would produce the most crucial piece of evidence that would tie the case together.

"I need assurances that if I give you 'the list,' you'll move me somewhere else, where my mother and I will be safe from these dangerous people. I'm scared for my life, Maged *beh,*" Camillia said, her eyes watering up with fear and despair.

Maged reassured her that the authorities would move her and her mother to another location, possibly another governorate or city in Egypt, where they could both start a new life with new identities. He emphasized the fact that if she refused to hand over the paper right now, he would make sure she would be locked up in prison for a very long time. Camillia glanced downwards, much like a guilty child who had just been caught stealing from a candy store. She was terrified, and yet her inner voice nagged at her to hand the list over to Maged. She wanted to relieve herself from the anxiety that had gripped her for the past two weeks, and she trusted this officer.

She also knew that moving to another city would give her and her mother a secure and more comfortable life. She had always wanted to move to Alexandria, a city that was very dear to her heart. She remembered how overjoyed she was when she visited the coastal city on a school trip when she was 14 years old. Ever since then, she had always dreamed of moving there. She wanted to be able to take those long strolls by the white sandy beaches, to breathe in the salty odor of the waves as they crashed against the rocks, causing the seawater to splash high up in the humid air.

She finally mustered the courage to express to Maged her desire to be relocated to Alexandria in exchange for handing over 'the list.' Maged suddenly stopped pacing and waited patiently for Camillia to finally hand him the piece of paper. He looked at her and nodded his head, trying to encourage her to make the right decision. She finally caved in and walked to her bedroom, closing the door gently behind her. Maged let out a sigh of relief, almost collapsing back onto the gray sofa. He had to restrain himself from jumping back to his feet with joy, feeling elated that he had finally managed to persuade his main witness to turn in the notorious 'list.'

Surely enough, he watched on as Camillia opened her bedroom door and walked out with a folded piece of paper in her hand. She walked toward him and finally handed him 'the list,' feeling relieved and at the same time fearful of what loomed ahead for her and her mother. Maged slipped on a pair of latex gloves and almost snatched the paper out of her hand, his eyes searching frantically for the one missing name that he needed to know. The unknown name was Osama Mansour. The name was unfamiliar to him, and he couldn't wait to run it through the national database system.

He carefully placed the piece of paper in a plastic bag and reassured Camillia one final time that she would be safe somewhere else with her mother and that he would personally make sure that they would be relocated to Alexandria. He also told her that she wouldn't be able to leave her apartment just yet and that staying put would guarantee her safety. With that being done, Maged ran down the stairs and headed directly to his office at the *Zamalek* police station.

He went directly to his office, not speaking to anyone on the way, feeling very uneasy, and looking around him so as not to run into Assem. He closed the door and switched his computer on, impatiently waiting to sign into the national data system using his security code. He typed in the name, Osama Mansour, and hit the search button. The search result showed several Egyptian men going by that same first and last name. He scanned the seemingly endless names, trying to see what these men did for a living and whether any of them had prior felonies or jail sentences on record. He found eight men with minor felonies and three who were already serving jail sentences in prisons across the country.

His eyes stopped scrolling down when he found 30 men named Osama Mansour serving in the police force, army, and navy. He printed out the list of 30 names and began scrutinizing each one. Eight of those men were actively serving in the police force all over the country, but only one of them was currently on active duty as a police officer in Cairo. Maged looked at the picture of the man very closely. His heart began beating very rapidly, and his mouth became as dry as a parched desert. It was Assem's face in the profile picture! Maged knew he had finally nailed the bastard! But he never knew that Assem had a hyphenated name. It was actually Osama Assem Mansour Ezzat, whereas Maged and all the police officers knew him by the name Assem Ezzat. Maged now realized why Camillia hadn't recognized Assem's name from the very beginning. Had she recognized his name, she would have reported it earlier in the investigation.

Maged now possessed all the hard evidence he needed to present to Rawan and Kamal in their meeting tomorrow morning. He had the proof to tie all five names on the list to the murder in Suite 55 and, by default, to the 'red dust' cartel's operation in Egypt. Armed with this substantial new information and the bagged evidence in his hand, Maged discreetly left the police station and headed to the forensics lab to present his evidence for forensic lab testing. The lab technicians told him they would notify him if they came up with anything significant. Maged told them not to report to anyone else but him and that the report was considered a classified document.

He then headed home, where he could plan his next move. He wanted the 'Code Red' task force to act swiftly but cautiously. The fact that Assem was being watched around the clock and that his car was being tracked sufficed in Maged's mind to reduce Assem's danger. Maged began pacing back and forth in his living room, his mind working through all the 'murder bytes,' sifting through all the information all at once. His train of thought was interrupted when he received a message from one of the secret agents watching Assem's apartment. The agent reported that Assem had just left his apartment and that his car was being tailed by an undercover officer. Maged told the secret agent to keep him abreast of where Assem was going.

It was nearing nine o'clock at night, and Maged had a lot of preparation to do for tomorrow's meeting. He had never been to the 'bunker' before and so he didn't know what to expect, but he knew it was a classified location, privy only to authorized national security personnel. He was going to have to present evidence that tied all five names to Mona's murder and the 'red dust' cartel's operation in Egypt, but he still had no murder suspects. He wondered if the murderer could have been Assem himself, or perhaps Marwan or Farida. It may have also been Murad or Demir, or someone else entirely, not yet known to the police.

Maged believed that by tailing Assem, Marwan, and Farida, the police could soon be led to Mona's killer.

But then Maged had an epiphany. *None of them could actually know who the murderer was*, he thought to himself. Just then he received a call from the agent tailing Assem, who told him that Assem had just parked his car in front of the *Zamalek* police station. Maged had no idea why Assem would be at the police station at this time of the night.

But he now had tomorrow's meeting to worry about.

Chapter Twenty-Seven
'The Bunker'

Maged had to follow the GPS on his phone to get to the meeting, which was not somewhere remote in the desert as he had initially suspected. The meeting was going to take place in the very heart of downtown Cairo, in an old historic mansion that once belonged to Tawfik Helmy *Pasha.* The ornate mansion was now being renovated to welcome locals and tourists as a historic art gallery, showcasing oil paintings and antiques dating back from the forties and fifties. Maged parked his car two blocks away and decided to walk, taking in the splendor of downtown Cairo. History was always Maged's favorite subject in school, and he was repeatedly told by his history teacher that anyone who seeks true knowledge must become an avid history reader.

Once he reached the designated location, he was fascinated by the regal façade of the mansion. Four winged lions with sharp fangs faced the main entrance, while eight marble columns decorated with dragons and eagle heads gave visitors an ominous welcome. Maged continued walking down a long dirt pathway, as he was instructed, until he reached the back entrance to the mansion. Behind the green scaffolding, he was greeted by two secret agents who escorted him down two flights of stairs to the basement, where he met agent Rawan and officer Kamal. Maged was taken aback by what he saw in the huge basement and realized why they referred to this location as the 'bunker.' In contrast to the old historic façade of the mansion, he was now looking at the most advanced, wall-to-wall state-of-the-art satellite and surveillance equipment. He looked at Rawan in amazement as she walked toward the satellite screens that were beaming footage from across the world in real time.

"Officer Maged, welcome to the 'bunker,' where our task force could not only track down criminals all over the world in real time but also trace dark web activity and disrupt illegal crypto-drug market activity. This 'bunker' is especially equipped to engage in cyber-drug wars of the fifth generation. It is one of three in the entire world. Needless to say, this is my home on most weekdays, where I perfect my abilities and skills," Rawan explained, her monotone voice beaming with pride.

"It is a work of art, much like the mansion it is nestled in," Maged said, hurriedly taking a seat at the long black conference table situated on one end of the open space. He scanned the space quickly, looking at the plain gray concrete flooring and the soundproof cladded walls.

"Officer Maged, we're running out of time on this case. It's already been two weeks," Kamal interjected, in a gesture to quickly get to business. "Public opinion is in uproar that your task force hasn't arrested Mona's killer yet, and the public prosecutor is demanding an immediate arrest to quell public fears. Of course, and as expected, some international media channels are deliberately putting Mona's unsolved murder front and center in their international news coverage," Kamal said, taking a seat opposite Maged.

"And that's exactly why I asked that this 'Code Red' task force be formed. I am here today to give you the pieces of the puzzle that will connect the five names on 'the list' to Mona El Safty's murder," Maged said, wanting to delve right into the evidence he had pieced together the day before.

"Tell us what you have," Rawan said, taking a seat at the table and flipping open her laptop.

"Camillia finally gave me the list of names! The five names on the list are Farida El-Leithy, Marwan El Meligy, Demir Dogan, Murad Abdel Hamid, and Osama Mansour, aka Assem Ezzat!" Maged said, his voice getting louder in an effort to put emphasis on the last name. "So, besides the voice recordings that I have of the conversations between Farida and Marwan, which directly implicate Assem, I now also have hard evidence that ties these five people to the murder site and to the 'red dust' cartel,"

Maged said, fighting the urge to get up and start his fetish of pacing back and forth.

"This is a major development in the case, Officer Maged!" Kamal said, his facial muscles now looking more relaxed. Maged could tell that Kamal was fighting his own urge to light a cigarette, but that he was restraining himself because of the smoke detectors that lined the concrete ceiling. Maged also noticed that there were no windows, making the basement look like a concrete vault.

"Great! Now I will explain what I have found out during the past 48 hours about how this particular drug cartel operates," agent Rawan said, walking toward one of the walls, which suddenly switched from displaying real-time satellite imagery to becoming a huge web interface. "Let me begin by explaining how the 'red dust' cartel has managed to elude the Interpol for so long. They use what is known as crypto-drug markets. In short, these are anonymous dark net sites which broker the purchase and sale of domestic and international illegal drug substances," Rawan explained as she tapped the web interface, her voice projecting confidence and knowledge.

"Are you saying we can't track their bitcoin dealings? Is there any way we could disrupt their 'chain-hopping' mechanism of moving between crypto-currencies in order to avoid being tracked?" Kamal asked, looking very alert and focused on what Rawan was saying.

"No, that's not what I'm saying. Actually, law enforcement can track and seize illegal funds at the speed of the internet precisely because criminals transfer funds without a bank's permission. So, it is traceable. And that's where my role comes in," Rawan continued, her composure making Maged relax and have more confidence in 'Code Red' mission's success.

"I'm not very familiar with dark net markets and their modes of operation," Maged interjected, looking slightly uncomfortable as he shifted his body in his chair. "But I did question Farida about how she gets paid for her operations in Egypt. She explained that she gets bitcoin payments sent to her bank account in Zurich. I will send you her bank account details so you could begin your trace from there," Maged said, nodding his head toward Rawan.

Rawan assured both Maged and Kamal that she was working very closely with other intelligence agents and computer engineers to develop and operate the most advanced 'quantum' computer, which would have the ability to solve algorithms that no other conventional computer could ever solve.

"We have just finalized our own Egyptian 'quantum' computer which has the ability to crack bitcoin codes and unlock crypto-wallets all over the globe," Rawan explained, as she confidently walked toward the table and took her seat. "It is only a matter of a few days before we could help Interpol unlock bitcoin codes and seize all 'red dust' crypto-wallets," she added, smiling with pride.

Kamal stood up and walked toward the huge web interface, tapping on it twice to switch it back to satellite imagery. He enlarged the map using both hands until he zeroed in on Eastern Europe.

"That's wonderful to hear, agent Rawan. Now, this is how I believe the 'red dust' is being smuggled from the point of origin to the point of destination," he said, as he began tracing an invisible line with his pointer finger from Afghanistan, through the Balkan countries, and into southeastern Europe.

Maged inquired about the exact point of manufacture, but Kamal seemed hesitant to answer. Kamal explained that Turkey wasn't known to be a narcotics manufacturing country but that it served as a distribution hub for countries in Western Europe and North Africa. Kamal surmised that the 'red dust' coming from Port Mersin, Turkey, was being manufactured in a country somewhere in southeastern Europe, close to Turkey. He assured Rawan and Maged that he was working with the best intelligence minds in the country as well as Interpol to pinpoint the exact manufacturing location.

Kamal added that while Afghanistan was notorious for manufacturing opioids, he didn't think it was the only country involved in manufacturing the 'red dust.' He explained how 'red dust' was used as an odorless base and that Afghanistan lacked the necessary equipment and facilities to produce this type of advanced illegal substance, which was later mixed with other hallucinogens. He added that the fact that the 'red dust' was mixed with other substances made it all the more versatile and popular, not to mention lethal.

"But, Officer Maged, we don't want our pursuit of the drug cartel abroad to divert your attention from catching Mona's killer," officer Kamal continued, looking Maged straight in the eyes.

"Of course not, but our mission as a cohesive 'Code Red' task force is to find the killer and simultaneously obliterate the cartel, as we have discussed before. Don't worry about my police investigation here. As we speak, some of the best forensic science experts are extracting DNA evidence that will make us make an arrest very soon. I just don't want to make an arrest now in order not to jeopardize the success of our mission with Interpol abroad. Both objectives have to be fulfilled in tandem," Maged said, feeling confident in the success of his strategy.

With that being said, they all agreed to meet the following morning to meet Admiral Mostafa Soweilam, the final member of the 'Code Red' task force. He was expected to construct a plan to intercept the inbound shipment before it reached Egyptian waters. The admiral was going to be heading the naval squadron that would seize the 'red dust' from the container ship in the midst of the Mediterranean on New Year's Eve. Maged reaffirmed to Rawan and Kamal that he would make sure Farida would find out more information from Marwan about the maritime route which the big shipment was expected to take.

With that being said, Maged made his way out of the historical mansion, turning back to look at the four lions with sharp fangs. He shuddered as he walked to his car, quickly switching his phone back on. He immediately saw a blinking blue light, signaling that he had received a new message. The message was from the undercover agent who was tailing Assem.

The message read:

'I have been trying to reach you! Assem went to the Zamalek police station last night, then took a microbus to Camillia's apartment. He went upstairs to her flat for about 15 minutes. He then took a taxi back to his apartment.'

Maged felt extremely agitated by this message. He had no idea why Assem had visited Camillia's apartment last night, but he now realized that he was going to have to ask Assem why he had gone there. Both of them hadn't spoken a word to each other for the past week.

But it was now time for the two men to come face-to-face.

Chapter Twenty-Eight
'Tirana Ties'

While the 'Red Code' task force in Cairo was preparing for a showdown with the 'red dust' cartel in the Mediterranean, Armend Lika was in his villa in Tirana, counting the days till New Year's Eve. He desperately wanted to put an end to the nightmare that had unfolded in Cairo during the past two weeks. He believed that Mona's murder should have been executed with far more skill and professionalism, but what ensued was a murder that had gotten completely out of hand, and covering it up was proving to be even more costly and dangerous for the newly created and powerful 'red dust' cartel. Armend had never been involved in such a complicated drug operation before in any western European or North African country. He was used to supervising seamless operations, where every operator and 'lieutenant' knew their roles and carried out instructions without asking questions or ever daring to cross the line.

To complicate matters further, Armend began hearing complaints from some overseas operators that they were not getting paid on time and that some crypto-wallets were refusing to accept bitcoin deposits. Armend was extremely frustrated because it was unheard of in his extensive 'red dust' network that dark net brokers and operators would have trouble depositing or cashing out bitcoin payments. Armend knew something wasn't right, and he began to feel uneasy for the first time since the cartel's inception two years ago. He asked his confidant to contact Assem and make sure that any obstacles to the inbound shipment on New Year's Eve be resolved immediately. The shipment had to dock at Port Said harbor as scheduled, and Marwan had to have his men in place to oversee the handling of the entire operation.

With only five days till New Year's Eve, Armend's large villa in southern Tirana was buzzing with activity as ring operators from neighboring towns offered their assistance in exchange for hefty sums of money. Armend was feeling increasingly impatient to get the shipment safely onto Egyptian shores, knowing that this big shipment couldn't be risked or thwarted in any way. He also knew that his stature as drug lord of the 'red dust' cartel in Albania would be threatened and that he could possibly be voted out of his position by the consortium if he were to fail to deliver this shipment successfully. He was determined to maintain his power, and he was willing to take down anyone or anything that came in his way.

He decided to call a meeting that very evening in his villa, requesting the mandatory presence of all cartel lieutenants in the North African and Mediterranean regions. Armend wanted to know how the cartel could elude the Egyptian coast guards and navy, and make its way safely to Port Said harbor. The reports his cartel was getting from Cairo suggested that there was heightened activity happening there, which was exactly why no instructions had been given to Assem as to how the 'red dust' was to be distributed to local handlers in Cairo.

The cartel had decided that the safest place for the 'red dust' capsules would be in Assem's apartment until further notice. Armend also gave instructions to his operators in Cairo to mislead Marwan into thinking that a change of port was ordered for this final shipment of the year. The cartel had several reports indicating that Marwan and Farida had been meeting without being directed to do so, in clear violation of the cartel's mandate. Armend was therefore adamant that both operators be punished to some degree, but not to the extent that Murad and Demir had been totally eliminated after they became a liability. Armend was impressed by how his hired hitmen had done a wonderful job getting rid of them without leaving a trace.

With that positive thought, Armend sat back in his red leather armchair and admired the many tattoos on his arms, wanting to 'look the part' for this evening's meeting. He looked at his reflection in the huge black leather-encased mirror, smiling to himself as he stood tall in his black turtleneck and gray jeans. He was pleased to see that his brown beard had grown out, making him look older than his years, and how his pale green eyes gave him a sinister appearance. He liked how his crooked front tooth gave him character, and how the slash on his right brow reminded everyone that he was a street fighter who rightfully earned his position in the newly created cartel.

He walked to his round conference table and carefully reviewed the names of the nine attendees who were coming to his villa this evening. He also asked his assistant to provide a complete surveillance report on Officer Maged's movements in the coming five days. Armend was well aware from Assem's reports that Maged was shrewd, brave, and meticulous in his police work, which was going to make this upcoming shipment all the more challenging. That was exactly why every person on the attendee list tonight had a specific role to play in the shipment's delivery. Each one was going to be handsomely rewarded and recognized within the ranks of the 'red dust' cartel.

Armend's girlfriend, Nora, looked at him from afar with both fear and respect as he sat at the conference table. She knew she was lucky to be living in such extravagance, but she also paid a price for leading a very socially restricted life. She wasn't allowed to go out alone under any circumstances, and she had two bodyguards by her side at all times. Armend could sense that Nora was gazing at him. He continued scanning the nine names without looking up at her.

"What's the matter, Nora? Do you need anything, or has your cash run out?" he said, with clear sarcasm in his voice.

"No, just admiring you, my love," Nora responded, trying to mask the fear she continuously hid in her heart. She knew how angry Armend could get as she looked at the green bruise on her left leg.

"I don't want you around here tonight. I have a very important meeting. You could go spend the evening with your mother if you want," he said, finally looking up at her. He liked Nora a lot, but he learned to never put a woman before his business. Nora hurriedly agreed to his proposition, wanting to escape the villa's restrictive boundaries.

Two hours later, Armend sat impatiently in his conference room as the nine attendees filed in to take their seats at the long rectangular table. The room fell silent when he stood up to make an address, calling out the names of each of the attendees in a show of respect.

"Of course you all know why I have asked you to gather here today," he said, as he sat down and rested his arms on the table, interlacing his tattooed fingers under his chin. "Each one of you must partake in the success of this shipment to Egypt. If this shipment goes well, you will all rise in the ranks of the cartel," he said, lighting a cigar and exhaling the smoke in round, circular puffs.

The nine attendees murmured their affirmative acceptance of the challenge to partake in the shipment, swearing their allegiance to the cartel, and vowing to make sure the shipment got to the Egyptian shores on New Year's Eve as scheduled. Each attendee was going to be responsible for completing a specific chore in the operation, much like bolts on a conveyor belt. Armend watched on as his assistants gave each attendee a detailed explanation of the responsibilities they had to complete and the rewards they would each attain thereafter. Armend's aides then handed each attendee state-of-the-art Sky-phones and specific passwords that they would need to use to wipe out all evidence, such as messages, photos, and call logs, from their phones. They were also given modified tablets that they would need to use to access satellite imagery in real time, as well as small earpods and microphones to facilitate discreet communication.

Feeling satisfied with the results of the meeting, Armend stood up, in a clear sign that the meeting was now over. The attendees began to file out of the room in complete silence, keeping their heads down so as not to look Armend in the eye, as that was considered to be a gesture of disrespect in the cartel's modus operandi. Armend waited till he was finally alone in the room before he began discussions with his closest aides. As his lieutenant in Egypt, Assem had a major role to play in the success of the upcoming operation. His role was so vital that Armend had to give orders that Assem's every move be very closely monitored for the coming five days.

Armend rarely ever felt anxious, but today he felt something different in his gut. The reports coming in from Cairo confirmed that Mona's murder had stirred up the Egyptian police's investigation of the 'red dust' trade. Armend had learned from Assem that Maged and his task force had therefore easily established the connection between Mona's murder and the 'red dust' drug dealings in Egypt, given the trace evidence found in the deceased's toxicology report. It was very clear to Armend that Maged had now become the biggest obstacle to securing the delivery of the next shipment.

While Armend meticulously thought things over and prepared the logistics of the shipment, Nora had packed a small suitcase and was well on her way to her mother's house. She sat in the backseat of a black BMW X5, flanked by two bodyguards on each side. She dreamed of the day she would be able to drive herself around without the prying eyes of Armend's men. She was so desperate to break free from him that she sometimes thought of escaping to another city altogether, or better yet, to a neighboring country. She kept thinking of her cousin, who lived in Serbia, who might agree to give her temporary lodging, that's if she ever mastered the courage to actually risk her life and escape from Armend's villa.

But Nora had no idea that it wasn't only Armend's men who were watching her closely. Two other men were tailing her car in a silver Mercedes-Benz, both wearing sunglasses and heavy leather coats to keep them warm from the cold Albanian weather in December. The two men were determined to keep her in their sight no matter what the cost. They were given instructions to get as close to Nora as they possibly could without being detected in any way. They were trained to do just that. They were the best at what they did, and they were committed to maintaining their stellar track record.

They were trained to be invisible.

Chapter Twenty-Nine
'Gone for Good'

Camillia sat on the gray sofa with tears in her eyes as she watched her mother cough out blood on the soft white napkin. She began to remember how her mother would prepare white cheese sandwiches for her, and braid her long silky hair every morning before she left for school. Camillia stroked her mother's pepper gray hair and went to prepare some hot soup, feeling a sense of discomfort as she walked toward the small stove in the crammed up kitchen.

"*Hajja,* what kind of soup do you want me to prepare for you? I can make you some clear soup with peas or your favorite lentil soup. So, what will it be?" Camillia called out as she pulled out a medium-sized pot and began to chop up a small red onion.

"Anything is fine with me," her mother answered back with difficulty in a low, raspy voice. Nadia began coughing incessantly, the bloody sputum increasing in quantity till she was completely out of breath.

Camillia began to worry that she would need a doctor to pay them a home visit tonight. The fact that she couldn't leave the apartment was now becoming increasingly stifling, as her mother was now in dire need of medical attention. Camillia felt so frustrated and helpless in the small apartment that she finally decided to call Maged and request that her mother be granted a doctor's visit.

Camillia dialed Maged's number twice before he finally answered. "Hello, Maged *beh*! My mother is really sick! Could you send a doctor to come and check her up, please?" Camillia asked, her voice showing clear signs of panic and anxiety.

"What's the problem?" Maged asked, sensing that this wasn't an act on Camillia's part.

"She's coughing up blood, and her breathing has been worsening for the past few days," Camillia explained, her voice shaking with fear and anxiety.

"Alright, I will send a doctor tomorrow morning to see her. Don't even think about leaving your apartment," Maged said, his voice becoming harsh so as to dissuade her from even thinking about stepping outside.

Camillia's legs shook as she walked back to the kitchen to continue making the lentil soup, which was her mother's favorite during the winter months.

"Do you want anything else besides the soup?" Camillia asked as she stirred the soup and tasted it to make sure she hadn't added too much salt.

Camillia waited for her mother to answer but heard no response. She then poured some soup into a glass cup and headed to her mother's small room. She looked at her mother and found her motionless, with her head slumped to one side and her eyes half open. Camillia dropped the glass cup to the floor and began sobbing hysterically as she began to shake her mother's arms, hoping to bring her back to life.

Her hands trembled as she picked up her phone and dialed Maged's number, her heart heavy with feelings of anger, sadness, and frustration for not being able to save her mother's life in time.

"Maged *beh*!" Camillia sobbed, her face wet with warm tears that kept rolling down her cheeks.

"What's the matter, Camillia? Is your mother alright?" he asked with genuine concern and anxiety.

"She's dead! My mother is dead!" Camillia screamed into the phone as she kept pulling at her clothes.

Maged could feel Camillia's sadness, and it made him wish he had sent the doctor right away. Trying to put his emotions aside, he cleared his throat and told Camillia to calm down and that her mother is in a much better place now.

"Definitely, she's in a better place now!" Camillia said with sarcasm, trying to make Maged feel guilty for not sending a doctor sooner and for preventing her from going out of her apartment.

"We are doing what we're doing to protect you, Camillia. You are the main witness in a murder trial that involves very dangerous people. They may try to harm you if you venture outside your apartment," Maged said, trying to practice some damage control.

"So will you even allow me to bury my mother?" Camillia asked, her anger boiling over now.

Maged assured her that she would be allowed to attend her mother's burial, provided that they escorted her to the burial site and back to her apartment. Camillia thanked him and hung up the phone, slapping her face repeatedly, her heart pounding with deep sadness, feeling so alone in this world. She knew her life would never be the same without the presence of her mother and that she had to find a way to go back to work or be moved to another city altogether, as Maged had previously promised her. She didn't care anymore if it was Alexandria, she just needed to get out of the confines of her claustrophobic apartment and into the hustle and bustle of everyday life outside.

Camillia spent the entire night crying next to her mother's body until the crack of dawn. She got dressed in a long black skirt, a black long sleeved top, and a heavy black wool shawl and readied herself for the burial, which was to take place by noon. She couldn't eat or even drink water due to the grief that seemed to be choking her throat. She looked at herself in a small broken mirror that hung on the gray wall, only to see the face of someone she didn't recognize anymore. Her face was pale, with heavy bags under her eyes, and her lips were cracked and dry. She had nobody now to offer her solace or even listen to her when she was angry or frustrated at life. She sat on the gray sofa, waiting to hear a knock on the door. She wanted her mother to be buried with the honor and dignity that she deserved.

Maged arrived a few hours later to Camillia's apartment in a police car accompanied by two officers, armed with weapons and wearing heavy protective gear. Camillia's mother's body was transported to a nearby public hospital, where her lifeless body was washed with soap and scented water, then wrapped in a white cotton shroud, and readied for burial. Camillia was transported in a police van with two male police officers and two female officers. She attended the *ghusl* and watched as her mother's body was being wrapped in the seamless cloth and tied at the head and feet. Camillia shuddered as she began to feel increasingly suffocated, as if she herself were the one being wrapped and tied up.

Nadia's body was then taken to the burial site, where her body was removed out of the wooden casket and laid to rest in a small underground chamber. Camillia couldn't help sobbing loudly, slapping her face with her palms as she bid her mother farewell. She was beginning to feel dizzy as she stood with the two female police officers on one side, while Maged and the two male officers stood on the other side. Maged's eyes kept scanning the surroundings, making sure nobody came close to Camillia during the burial procedure. A *sheikh* was reciting verses from the Quran, after which all attendees began noon prayers.

Maged and the two male officers kept a close eye on Camillia as she prayed, flanked by the two female officers on either side. Once she was done praying, Camillia asked to speak to Maged alone in order to thank him for allowing her to leave her apartment for the burial procedure. She looked at him with tears streaming down her face, her head pounding from the bad headache she had as a result of all the crying she had done all day.

Suddenly, Camillia's face became contorted in anguish and pain, and she seemed to be losing her balance. Maged didn't understand what was happening until he saw the gunshot wound to the side of her forehead! He threw himself onto her, rushing to shield her with his body, but it was too late. Camillia began falling to the ground, blood oozing down her face from the gunshot wound. She felt warm and peaceful inside, as her last thought was a hazy image of herself and her mother walking down a sandy beach in Alexandria, laughing together as they kicked the waves with their bare feet.

Maged couldn't believe what he was witnessing as he shouted for all the officers to pursue the hitman who had just killed Camillia. The shooter had obviously used a gun silencer to detract the police from his shooting position. Maged quickly radioed in for backup, asking all officers in the area to rush to the scene of the crime. He looked around in a frenzy and spotted a three-story building to the right of the burial site, which was still under construction. He was sure that that was the vantage point the assassin had used to shoot Camillia.

He instinctively ran toward the building, followed by the officers, who quickly surrounded the building in case the hitman was still holed up inside. Maged held his handgun tightly and began to slowly ascend the broken concrete staircase, signaling for the officers to follow suit. They began searching every floor for the shooter, only to find empty steel barrels and sacks of cement strewn everywhere. He began to move at a quicker pace, stopping suddenly when he heard a faint noise at the far end of the second floor. He motioned for the officers to protect his back as he slowly made his way toward the source of the sound. He was certain the shooter was hiding behind a barrel when he caught a glimpse of black fabric. He motioned for two officers to approach the barrel with him, and all three of them pointed their guns in unison at the barrel.

"Don't shoot! Please! I will come out!" the shooter said, sounding like a cornered prey.

Maged told him to come out from behind the barrel with his hands up in the air or else they would shoot to kill. The shooter did as he was told and stood up slowly with his arms up. Maged rushed to him, holding him firmly by the hands, while the officers aggressively handcuffed him.

"Who do you work for?" Maged shouted at him angrily, feeling guilty that he couldn't protect Camillia's life as he had promised her. He had to restrain himself from punching the shooter in the face.

"They'll kill me! Even if you jail me, they'll find me and kill me!" the shooter pleaded.

"You're dead anyway! Speak up now or I will make sure you have a speedy death sentence!" Maged answered back as he looked the shooter in the eyes.

"They told me to do it! They told me to shoot her in exchange for a lot of cash!" the shooter said, his face covered with cement powder.

"Who told you to kill her?" Maged asked, trying his best to extract the information before the shooter could regain his composure.

"Those powerful people! They told me to do it! They told me she had to pay the price for speaking up! That's all I know! I swear!" the shooter said.

Maged told the officers to take the shooter to the nearest police station, making sure they didn't take him to the *Zamalek* station, where Assem could attempt to interrogate him and change the facts of the confession. By that time, three police cars had appeared for backup, providing the much-needed heavy security to escort the killer.

A few minutes after that, Maged's nemesis arrived at the scene of the crime, looking out of breath and distraught.

"They killed her! I can't believe Camillia was shot after all we did to protect her!" Assem said, pretending to mean what he was saying. "They waited for her to leave her house! The bastards were watching her every move!" Assem shouted, slapping his thighs as he spoke.

Maged had to look away to restrain himself from showing the spite he felt for the man in front of him. He clenched his fist, digging his nails into his skin, in an effort to control his rage. Maged knew this was the worst time for him to lose control of his emotions, and he desperately wanted to see Assem shackled in handcuffs, much like the killer had just been a few minutes earlier.

"Yes! They killed her Assem!" Maged said, trying his best to play along. "But they'll pay the price for this and for everything else they've done," Maged continued, his voice now strong and full of patriotism.

"Do you really think we'll bring this cartel down?" Assem asked, looking at Maged in the eyes.

"Since when have we ever lost a war?" Maged answered back, returning the stare with a smile.

"But this cartel is very well connected!" Assem said, in an effort to extract any information he could about Maged's next move.

"Assem, when we joined the police force, we swore to uphold the law and protect the people of this country. That's exactly what I'll do," Maged responded with restraint, looking directly at Assem.

"Of course! They will never win! Over my dead body!" Assem answered back.

"Exactly!" Maged responded as he clenched his fist.

Chapter Thirty
'Profile of a Killer'

Maged left Assem at the scene of the crime and headed directly to his office at the *Zamalek* police station. He gathered all the evidence he had collected on Mona's murder and the 'red dust' cartel over the past 16 days and went to his apartment to begin his 'war room' preparations. Images of Camillia's bloodied face kept haunting him wherever he went. No matter how hard he tried to pace back and forth around his dining room table, he couldn't shake off the guilt he felt for her death. He had promised to keep her safe but he had ultimately failed to keep her alive.

With only four days left till New Year's Eve, Maged knew he had to focus now more than ever before. He understood that the cartel was trying to cause the greatest psychological damage possible in an effort to make him lose his focus and concentration. They wanted to distract him from the most crucial hours remaining till the big shipment sailed in. That's precisely why Maged wanted to go to the 'bunker' this afternoon with heightened awareness and preparation for the herculean mission ahead of him. But no matter how hard he tried to focus on piecing his material and evidence together for the meeting today, Camillia's face would appear in his mind and blind his concentration, as if she were begging for his undivided attention.

Maged was impatiently waiting for the forensic report, especially the DNA extraction from 'the list.' He still hadn't received the report and was frustrated that it was taking so long. He decided to head to the forensics lab right away to inquire about the results, knowing that he owed it to Camillia, who paid the ultimate price for speaking out to police, as well as to Mona, who had equally paid the ultimate price for wanting to expose this nefarious cartel.

With only three hours left before his meeting with the 'Code Red' task force, Maged wanted to make every minute count. He quickly spread all his case evidence around the living room, pasting all the documents, confessions, and floor maps of the Imperial Hotel, as well as his 'murder bytes' onto the walls and bare floor. He stood back and tried to create a cohesive narrative of the entire case in his mind. He then pulled out his phone and began to record himself speaking as he meticulously pieced together all the evidence he had collected, as if he were in a courtroom presenting his case before a judge. He wanted to present airtight evidence against Assem, Farida, and Marwan and to explain Murad and Demir's roles in the cartel's operations. But more importantly, as a police officer, Maged had to find Mona's killer. He left his apartment in a rush and headed to the forensics lab.

"Maged, we're glad you're here, we were just about to call you," one of the lab technicians said, his voice not giving anything away.

"What do you have for me?" Maged asked, with desperation in his voice, wanting crucial information to be presented in his meeting.

"We did find a single fingerprint that didn't belong to the deceased," the same technician said.

"Hand me what you've got! I need to run it through our database now!" Maged said, his voice loud and strong.

"We already gave it to Assem. He just left half an hour ago!" the other technician said, thinking Maged would be pleased to hear that.

"What? Assem! I told you not to divulge any information to anybody working the case, except me!" Maged shouted, his voice echoing in the building's hallway. He was so angry that he made a fist and dug his nails into his palm.

"Calm down! We have exclusive evidence for you, which we didn't give to him!" one of the technicians said hurriedly. "We managed to extract DNA evidence from the few gray hairs found in one of the sinks in the suite. And we also managed to find a partial fingerprint on the shirt button you turned in. It was the same fingerprint as the one we extracted from the piece of paper!" the technician said, looking pleased with himself.

"Hand me your report immediately!" Maged demanded, looking at both technicians with resolve.

One of the technicians hurried to his desk and handed Maged a red folder, which the police officer immediately opened. He began reading the report, his eyes scanning the sentences quickly. Maged hurried back to the police station to run the partial fingerprint into the national database, his heart beating very rapidly now, desperate to know the identity of the person who had killed Mona. He was desperate to tie the whole case together before heading to his meeting with the admiral, Rawan, and Kamal.

He quickly entered all the DNA evidence into the system himself, not trusting anyone at this crucial moment in time. He wanted answers, and he wanted them now. His fingers trembled as he carefully typed in the information, pressing the enter button, and praying for a match to appear on his computer screen. He waited for what seemed to be an eternity before a name finally appeared before his eyes.

He froze in his seat. He couldn't believe it!

It was the one person he had never suspected from the start. The one person who was at the scene of the crime and watched him from afar. The one person nobody would have thought would have a motive to kill Mona. It was the one person who could have orchestrated the seamless removal of the deceased's corpse from Suite 55 to the dumpster outside the posh hotel and gone unnoticed.

The fingerprint belonged to Hamed Mohamed Abdallah, aka Mr. Hamed. Armed with this incriminating new information, Maged drove directly to his meeting, his mind working fervently to piece together the murder puzzle. He stopped his car near the curb and pulled out his phone to record a voice note. He pressed the red record button and laid out his case against Hamed, the Housekeeping Manager:

'Hamed could be working with the 'red dust' cartel, facilitating their meetings in the suites on the fifth floor of the Imperial Hotel in Zamalek, especially Suite 55, where some of their most shady operations take place. Hamed knew that Mona was going to hand over very sensitive information to the Maitre D' in the Maharaja Indian restaurant at nine o'clock on the night of the murder. He instructed the maître D' to slip her a note inside the bills directing her to go upstairs to Suite 55 for a meeting with someone who would listen to her explosive journalistic story about the 'red dust' cartel and their powerful connections in Egypt.'

'Assem, is, with no doubt in my mind, the mystery person who had sent Mona text messages instructing her to go to the Indian restaurant. Hamed may have met Mona inside Suite 55 and tried to strike a deal with her so that she accepts a certain amount of money in exchange for handing him 'the list' and refraining from publishing or exposing any material about the 'red dust' cartel. Mona refused Hamed's proposition, and a heated argument ensued. Mona initially thought Hamed was an intelligence officer who was meeting her to listen to her evidence; therefore, she was extremely angered by his proposal. She may have threatened him using the evidence she had collected in her investigation, as well as threatening to expose 'the list' in her possession.'

'Hamed may have asked to look at 'the list,' but Mona refused, leaving him with no other alternative except to discreetly placate her by slipping a dose of 'red dust' into her drink. She began to get drowsy and suspected that he had put something in her drink. She asked to use the bathroom, dropping the list on purpose on the floor and shoving it under the curtain. She left her fingerprints all over the bathroom's countertop and faucets, then exited the bathroom, sitting on the armchair by the oval table.'

'Hamed may have surprised her by hitting her with a blunt object to the side of her forehead. She touched her wound and tried to get up, leaving traces of her blood on the upholstered armchair. In her effort to escape, drops of her blood fell to the carpet underneath the chair. She then tried to steady herself by touching the wall, leaving traces of her blood on the wallpaper above the side table. She most likely fell onto the bed, staining the bed covers, forcing Hamed to strip the bedding in an effort to conceal her DNA evidence.'

'He had all the cleaning detergents ready, and he fervently tried to scrub the stains off the armchair, the carpet, and the wallpaper. Hamed may have then wrapped Mona's body inside the bed covers and placed her body inside a housekeeping trolley, which was probably already inside the suite. He could have used the staff elevator to transport the trolley downstairs and out to the dumpster on the backstreet of the hotel, under the guise that the trolley contained garbage bags.'

Maged replayed his voice recording, feeling that he had pieced together a plausible scenario of how Mona was murdered in Suite 55. But something didn't feel right to him. The scenario felt too well orchestrated. He started his ignition and continued driving to the 'bunker.' What weighed heavily on his mind now was that Hamed was still a free man, and that Assem now knew that Hamed's identity had been revealed after a long and painstaking effort by the forensics lab. Images of Camillia's bloodied forehead continued to hound him. He parked his car two kilometers away from the old mansion and walked there on foot, rehearsing what he was about to tell the 'Code Red' task force. As he entered the gateway to the old mansion, he looked at the four sculptured lions with sharp fangs, hoping he would be capable of ending this case the way he wanted it to end. He continued walking toward the back of the mansion and was met by two agents behind the green scaffolding, exactly like he had been the previous time. They escorted him to the basement, where Rawan and Kamal were seated at the table waiting for him. He felt the same sense of awe as he entered the basement, mixed with sudden disappointment when he didn't spot Admiral Mostafa.

"The admiral will be here in four minutes. Welcome back to the 'Bunker,' Officer Maged," Rawan said, her voice projecting the usual air of confidence.

Chapter Thirty-One
'The Admiral'

"I'm glad the admiral will join us because I have very important news," Maged answered back, his own voice carrying a hint of mischief mixed with slight doubt.

"What do you have for us?" Admiral Mostafa asked as he walked into the basement with a stride of confidence. He extended his hand to Officer Maged, greeted Rawan and Kamal, and then walked directly to the satellite images beaming from all four walls. The admiral was about 60 years of age, medium height, with hazel eyes and a full head of graying hair. He exuded an air of optimism mixed with experience.

"It's an honor to meet you, Admiral Mostafa," Maged said, as he stood up in a show of respect for the admiral. "But before we discuss the maritime operation in the Mediterranean, I need to talk about what happened today. Camillia was killed by a hitman as she attended her mother's burial this afternoon," Maged said, looking downward in a show of respect for the deceased, mixed with guilt for not being able to protect her. "We managed to catch the shooter, who had used a building under construction as his shooting location. The shooter admitted to being hired by powerful people who promised him a lot of money if he killed Camillia," Maged explained, as he began to pace the concrete floor.

"That's the final nail in their coffin," Kamal said, as he calmly looked at the ceiling, his hands interlaced behind his head.

"Hamed, the Housekeeping Manager, appears to be Mona's killer. His fingerprint was found on 'the list,' his DNA was extracted from a few gray strands found in one of the bathroom sinks in the suite, as well as a partial fingerprint found on a shirt button found at the scene," Maged continued.

"I want to play back a voice recording I just made as I was driving here. I tried to piece together how Mona's murder may have happened and how Hamed could have been able to dispose of the body without being detected," Maged continued.

Maged played his recording and watched the faces of the three attendees as they listened intently to his analysis of what happened on the night of Mona's murder.

"It sounds plausible," Kamal said, looking directly at Maged. "But what makes you so sure it was Hamed? It could have been someone else who planted Hamed's shirt button in the suite along with a few of his gray strands in the sink," Kamal continued. "Don't forget he's the housekeeping manager and he may have entered the suite on several occasions to inspect its cleanliness before the crime was committed," Kamal continued, making Maged feel uneasy.

"With all due respect, Kamal *beh*, I am definitely taking that into consideration. I checked the cameras in the hallway, which only records footage for 48 hours at a time. The footage wasn't tampered with. Hamed wasn't seen in the footage the morning the police were there, which means that he could have been in the suite the night of the murder," Maged explained.

"But did you see him in the footage actually enter Suite 55, the night of the murder?" Kamal continued, trying to press Maged for definitive answers.

"I went over the camera footage repeatedly. He did enter the Suite adjacent to Suite 55. I went to the Imperial Hotel myself several times, the last time being two days ago. I looked at the floor plan of the fifth floor and found that Suite 55 had a connecting door to Suite 53," Maged explained.

"You only found out about this connecting door two days ago?" Rawan asked, looking quizzically at Maged.

"When the police went to the crime scene, the connecting door was completely concealed with wooden paneling, obviously in an effort to throw off the investigating team. I went to Suite 55 two days ago and was able to locate the door opening. My team and I detected evidence of an adhesive substance in the wood paneling," Maged explained.

"We congratulate you on your effort, Officer Maged," the admiral said. "But what about Assem? He obviously now knows that you have discovered Hamed's fingerprints and that you also have Camillia's shooter in custody. How are you planning to deal with him for the remaining four days?" the admiral asked, rubbing his chin, his hazel eyes ablaze with curiosity.

"I have to pretend that I know nothing about his involvement with the 'red dust' cartel. That's the only way we could end this case the way we want it to. But there is something I need to ask him," Maged continued, still pacing the concrete floor. "I need to know why he went to Camillia's apartment the night before she was killed. Now that she's gone, I have no way to verify what he says anyway," Maged said, looking up to face his audience.

"That's an important question, but you won't get a truthful answer. Now I believe it's time for you to see how I plan to lead the navy squadron that will intercept this shipment. With less than four days remaining, the stakes are very high, and we have to plan our every move with exact precision. The four of us will have to be here for the entire day on New Year's Eve. Together we will coordinate the agents on the ground, the coastguard personnel, navy officers at sea, and forces in the air," the admiral said, his tone exuding expertise and leadership.

The admiral began to explain how the interception and impounding of the container ship would take place, highlighting the joint cooperation between the coast guards and the navy. Maged sensed that the admiral didn't disclose his entire plan, preferring to keep some parts under wraps till New Year's Eve.

"I will be responsible for disrupting their satellite communication and any communication equipment they will be using that day. I already have a team of three communication experts assisting me on that," Rawan said. "Disrupting their communication will be a key success factor for us.

Without their communication capability, all their efforts will be rendered obsolete," Rawan said, as she shivered in the air-conditioned basement.

"As for me, several agents are already in their positions, waiting for instructions. I assure you that we have patriotic undercover agents ready to serve our country," Kamal said, looking past Rawan's head, as if staring into the faraway distance. "I have devised a covert plan that will succeed to help our agents and Interpol bring down this cartel once and for all," Kamal continued, speaking slowly, as if he was playing out his strategy in slow motion in his mind.

They continued to discuss their plan for New Year's Eve, each member laying out as much detail as possible. The admiral asked Maged whether he had managed to get Marwan to divulge more information about the shipment's route. Maged told him that Farida was supposed to meet Marwan yesterday but that he seemed to be avoiding having any contact with her for the past three days.

"I'm afraid that the cartel has been watching Farida and Marwan too closely during this past week. Assem is under strict surveillance from both sides too. I am sure the cartel has me under very close watch now too," Maged said, as he sat down, his legs getting tired from pacing back and forth.

"What makes you say that?" Kamal asked, finally breaking his gazing trance, looking Maged straight in the face.

"It comes without question that Assem has already relayed to them everything that's happening here. I am a formidable obstacle to their shipment. They are probably planning how to kill me, as we speak," Maged continued, his face showing signs of stress and fatigue.

"That is a huge probability and something you need to take very seriously," Kamal said, looking away again. "I suggest you change your appearance in the coming few days, and consider moving out of your apartment till this operation is over," Kamal continued.

"I think you should stay here!" Rawan interjected. "The 'bunker' is actually your safest hideout. You can review the satellite feed in real time and get prepared for the final showdown," she said, pulling her shawl tightly around her shoulders.

Maged mulled over Rawan's proposal and realized that it was indeed his safest hiding place. He was sure the cartel would do everything in its power to get him out of the picture during the coming three days. Staying in the 'bunker' would not only offer him cover, but it would also make him focus on nothing else but their impending operation in the coming 72 hours.

"I think I will accept your offer, agent Rawan," Maged said. "But I will need to go back to my apartment to grab some belongings."

"Don't worry, Maged, give me the keys to your apartment, and I will have someone go get what you need," Kamal answered with confidence, his eyes looking past Maged's head.

The admiral looked at all three of them and nodded his head in a show of approval. He then got up and walked to the live satellite images beaming on the massive screens. He enlarged the map, zooming in on the Mediterranean Sea.

"We don't know where this shipment will be sailing from or where it will be docking. But rest assured, we will be waiting for them," he said, pointing at the images with his pointer finger.

"Admiral Mostafa, it was indeed an honor meeting you today," Maged said, as the admiral began to walk out of the basement. Maged felt an overwhelming sense of pride with the advances the navy had achieved, particularly during the past seven years. "I am sure this operation is the end of this cartel forever." The admiral shot him an affirmative look as he was escorted out of the 'bunker' by two secret agents.

Rawan and Kamal began stacking up their folders, bidding Maged farewell and assuring him that the 'bunker' had 24/7 surveillance from secret agents in case he needed anything in the coming three days. Maged was left to his own devices as he looked at the satellite images staring at him from all four walls of the basement. Maged then realized he had left his phone charger in his car and that his battery was about to die out. He walked toward the basement door to head out to his car and was surprised that the door was locked from the outside. He knocked three times to alert the agents on guard outside.

Nobody responded.

Chapter Thirty-Two
'Less than 72 Hours'

Armend couldn't sleep all night. He wasn't used to sleeping in his king-size bed alone, without Nora's warmth by his side. He missed her constant nagging and the fear that he saw in her eyes whenever he criticized anything she said or did. But it wasn't only Nora that he longed for. He longed for something new and thrilling in his life, so much so that he began to consider boarding the container ship all the way to Egypt. He wanted to be aboard the container ship when it docked at Port Said harbor, especially as Assem's men unloaded the 'red dust.' He wanted to witness that euphoric moment as it unfolded.

He knew that it was an irrational idea that would most likely cost him his life along with his drug lord status within the cartel, but he felt a maddening sense of bravery wash over him. He knew he would soon end up being killed or imprisoned anyway, so he wanted to choose his own fate for himself. The fact that this shipment was so lucrative for him and for the entire 'red dust' cartel in Albania made him fear failure more than ever before. That's precisely why he considered going on the journey himself to ensure the operation's success. Armend pulled out his Sky-phone and called Valon, his most trusted aide, to his villa in Tirana, spending the entire afternoon pouring over navigation maps and satellite imagery of the Mediterranean and the maritime route the ship was expected to take from Mersin to Port Said.

"Armend, I don't think you should do this! Going to Egypt will be disastrous for you and the entire cartel. You can't afford to take such a risk! The trip from Mersin to Port Said is about two full days at sea, which means you will have to leave in a few hours from now!" Valon said, looking alarmed by Armend's sudden, rash decision.

"I want to be there, Valon! I need to do this, and I need you to make sure that I will be safe. I want our top communication engineers and 'falcons' on the ground to be involved. I want this shipment to epitomize how we can all collaborate together. It will be the beginning of many successful future endeavors in North Africa!" Armend said this convincingly, making Valon begin to weigh the merits of his proposal.

"Armend, if you're really serious about this, then you'll have to pack your bag right now! I will have to send some of our best men with you. But if you want me to keep you safe, then we will have to make some adjustments to your initial plan," Valon said.

"What changes?" Armend asked, pacing around his large living room. "My plan is already in place; there's no time to change anything now!" Armend said, staring incredulously at Valon.

"Well, the fact that you're going to Egypt is a huge game-changer! We will have to change the sailing route. The ship will leave from Mersin, but we will change the docking location," Valon said, looking directly back at Armend. "We will dock in the port of Alexandria instead of Port Said. That way we will mislead the Egyptian police and keep you safe!" Valon said, his bald head glistening from the beads of sweat.

Armend agreed to Valon's new plan, believing that a change of destination would decrease the chances of the shipment being tracked by Maged's taskforce, as well as the Egyptian coast guard and navy. Valon told him he would contact Assem immediately so that he would have enough time to prepare his men in Egypt for the new destination.

Armend rushed to his bedroom upstairs and began packing a small suitcase for the sailing journey. He had to depart for Mersin, in Turkey, in exactly two hours. Valon needed those two hours to alert Armend's pilot to prepare Armend's private jet for the one hour and 40 minutes' flight to Mersin. A rush of much-needed adrenaline surged through Armend's body as he packed his suitcase. He never realized that being the 'red dust' cartel's drug lord meant nothing to him if it didn't make him feel alive, where he lived life on the edge. Growing up on some of the poorest streets in Tirana required an intelligent mind and a well-built body, and Armend knew he was lucky to have been endowed with both.

He grabbed his phone to call Nora to tell her that he was leaving for Mersin by private jet in a couple of hours, then on to another country on board a container ship. She felt relieved that she could stay with her mother for a few more days and wished Armend the best of luck on his voyage. But deep down in Nora's heart, she wished nothing more than to be set free from the shackles of the life she had with him. All she ever really wanted was to enjoy his wealth, but she sorely needed her freedom. She was hoping she would live to see that day.

Two hours later, Armend was boarding his private jet. He wanted Valon to oversee the operation from Tirana, making sure Armend was safe and secure throughout his journey. Once Armend boarded his private jet, Valon immediately contacted Assem by encrypted text message, alerting him to prepare for the new 'red dust' destination, Alexandria. Armend had also decided that the 'red dust' powder wouldn't be packaged in the usual over-the-counter capsules, but rather stuffed into the chairs, cushions, and furniture aboard the container ship.

While Armend kicked off his new Adidas shoes and poured over satellite images of the weather forecast in the Mediterranean region, Maged had been staring all night at similar satellite images, which were blaring at him from all four walls in the 'bunker.' The agents outside the basement had finally heard Maged's knocks and had sent an officer to Maged's car to get his phone charger. Maged wanted to make sure his father's health was alright, given that the old man lived alone after the death of Maged's mother. He now lamented the fact that he didn't have a wife or a significant other, despite being in his late thirties. Being a police officer had always made him feel scared to get emotionally committed, preferring not to drag an innocent woman into his dangerous, unpredictable life.

Maged couldn't sleep an iota that night, tossing and turning inside the sleeping bag, anxious to hear from Rawan and Kamal the next morning.

The 'Code Red' task force had a little over 48 hours before the shipment was bound to sail from Port Mersin to Port Said, and Maged was certain the shipping route was going to be changed in an effort to throw off the Egyptian police. The admiral had assured them that he was more than prepared for that scenario and that all ports sailing to Egypt on New Year's Eve were being watched around the clock by intelligence agents as well as Interpol.

But being locked inside the 'bunker' was much more emotionally straining than Maged had anticipated. If it weren't for his wrist watch and his phone, he wouldn't have been able to tell the time outside. The 'bunker' felt like a cold, controlled lab, with lights blinking everywhere and satellite images beaming continuously. He had studied the maritime routes on the navigational images so well that he wished he was part of the navy squadron under the admiral's directives.

There was a sudden, hard knock at the door. The door swung open from the outside, and Kamal walked in, with Rawan following closely behind him. They had two white plastic bags with them.

"We thought you'd be hungry by now," Rawan said, already shivering as they unpacked the two bags in a hurry.

"I definitely am. Anything would do, thank you!" Maged said, joining them at the table.

They unwrapped the warm *foul, falafel,* and *tahini* round sandwiches, eating hungrily and trying not to drop any crumbs on the long table. Fifteen minutes later, the admiral joined them, dressed in casual pants, a heavy green sweater, and a maroon neck scarf. They sat quietly at the table for a moment, getting their minds geared up for the final stretch of the operation.

"Maged, have you received any news about Assem since Camillia's murder?" Kamal blurted out suddenly, in his now familiar cross-examination mode.

"My agents are following Assem around the clock, and I haven't heard anything new from them since yesterday," Maged answered back, noting and admiring Kamal's attention to detail, despite his odd, far-off gazes.

"We are certain the container ship will not dock at Port Said harbor," the admiral said, as he folded his arms across his chest. "Kamal and I have been checking with our agents abroad, and we have reports that the ship will be diverted elsewhere to try to throw us off," the admiral explained. "We are prepared for anything they might be thinking of doing. The navy squadron under my command and the coastguard have already been on very high alert for the past week," the admiral said, as he moved toward the satellite images.

Admiral Mostafa began describing in detail how his squadron would intercept the inbound container ship, emphasizing the role of two helicopters which would provide air cover and protection for the navy and coastguards. Rawan then explained that her team of highly trained computer intelligence agents had already disrupted several online funding networks used by the cartel and that they were hours away from launching their 'Quantum Computer.' She was certain that in a matter of hours, Interpol would be able to arrest the drug lord along with his entire cartel by tracing their online activities and satellite communication, ultimately blocking off all their funding channels.

Kamal took his turn giving a briefing on the latest integrated report he had received from intelligence agents on the ground in Turkey and in nearby countries, which suggested that the shipment was departing from Mersin on New Year's Eve, as scheduled. As Kamal spoke, he received a text message on his phone, after which he excused himself for a few minutes. Kamal then returned to the table with a triumphant look on his face.

"I just received a message that the main person of interest our intelligence officers have been tracking for the past two weeks, has just landed at an airport in Mersin, Turkey," Kamal said, looking at the others with excitement. "This means that our intelligence dragnet did an astounding job closing in on this man," Kamal said, his face flooded with pride, as he looked up at the ceiling.

"Can you reveal his identity?" Maged asked in a hurry, desperately wanting to know the name of their nemesis.

"There are some things better left unsaid, for now," Kamal responded, gazing sideways as if mesmerized by a faraway magical land.

Chapter Thirty-Three
'Dangerous Liaisons'

Armend sat in the back seat of a metallic navy blue sedan, making his way to a cabin near Port Mersin. He was being taken to a lodge, where he would stay for a few hours before boarding the container ship to Alexandria. With a little over 48 hours remaining, Armend sent a text message to Valon, making sure that all details were in place and that their plan was airtight. Armend looked outside his window, taking in the beauty of Mersin with its high skyscrapers, tall lush palm trees, and long sprawling coastline. He made a mental note to purchase a villa on the beach in one of the trendiest spots in Mersin, taking a liking to the coastal city. Not only did he want to own a beautiful new villa outside Tirana, but he also needed to whitewash some of the huge profits that he had accrued from dealing in 'red dust' over the past two years.

Once he arrived at the lodge, Armend was pleasantly surprised to find a hot meal placed on the center table. Knowing that the food on the ship wouldn't satisfy his insatiable appetite, he ate almost everything on the plates. He also knew he was going to be aboard the ship for a total of four days, two days on each leg of the journey, which made him direct his assistants to prepare extra food stocks to take on board.

Armend's mind then wandered to Maged, wanting to know what the police officer and his task force were planning now that Camillia had been killed. He called Valon, inquiring about the latest news coming out of Cairo, wanting to make sure that Assem had his men ready in Alexandria and that Marwan was still under the impression that Port Said was the docking harbor. Assem was also given directives to keep the 'red dust' capsules in his apartment till after New Year's Eve, in case there were any complications with the shipment.

He then texted Nora, wanting to make sure she was safe at her mother's house and that her needs were being taken care of there. He told her he had arrived in Mersin and that he was going on a four-day trip somewhere. He didn't specify where he was going, as he always feared she would betray him one day. Armend had learned over the years to never trust anyone with his business secrets, always preferring to keep those closest to him at arm's length.

Armend had no idea that Nora was being watched very closely for the past two days and that her every move and character trait had already been studied and repeatedly analyzed by some of the best psychoanalysts in the intelligence field. He also had no idea that when Nora hung up with him, she would be overcome by a deep sense of freedom and elation. So much so that she got dressed to go for a relaxing stroll around the block. The weather was cold in Tirana in December, but Nora wanted to make use of every minute she had to revel in her freedom. She wanted to feel the cold wind in her face and to greet strangers as they walked by, all of them oblivious to the fact that she was the girlfriend of one of the most notorious drug lords in Albania.

But not all of the strangers that Nora greeted were ignorant of who she was.

She walked till the end of the street, then took a right turn into a small nearby park. It was a cold day, so Nora continued walking to keep warm until she came to a small fountain. She was about to exit the park when she was approached by a medium height male wearing a heavy jacket and sunglasses, with the jacket hood covering his head. Nora heard him mumble something under his breath, but she couldn't hear exactly what he had said. She gave him a smile and walked away, only to hear him murmur something again.

"Hello? Do you need any help?" Nora asked, pulling her jacket tightly around her chest as the wind picked up.

"Hello, I'm looking for a woman who lives around here, but I don't know her exact address," the man responded in English, smiling warmly.

"What's her name? I might be able to ask around for you," Nora said, noting his strange accent. She thought he was a lost tourist.

The man pulled a note from his pocket and handed the paper to Nora, which she then opened and read. She froze in her spot, not knowing how to react to what she had just read. She began to feel anxious, glancing left and right to make sure she wasn't being followed by Armend's bodyguards. She looked at the man and nodded her head, pointing her finger to the end of the road, as if giving him directions.

"How do I know you're for real and not someone from his side?" Nora asked, shifting her weight from one foot to the other.

"You'll get no jail time. You'll be free," the man said, as he smiled casually, pointing left and right, as if asking for directions. "He's in Mersin, then leaving on a trip, right? Just nod your head, then walk away," the man instructed her in a confident tone.

Nora nodded her head, smiled, and then walked away with a mixed sense of fear and elation. She couldn't believe what had just happened. The paper she just read said it all. Whomever this foreign man worked for clearly knew everything about Armend. All she needed to do was to confirm that he was in Mersin and that he was leaving on a journey somewhere. It was that simple, but it could open up a whole new world of opportunities for her. She wanted to be free from Armend for the rest of her life, and this stranger had just presented her with the chance she had been waiting for.

As Nora walked back to her mother's house, Armend boarded the furniture container ship headed for Alexandria. He felt the familiar surge of adrenaline run through his body as he sat in the small back room, which had been carefully prepared for his journey. As the container ship began sailing out to sea, Armend immediately pulled out his laptop and Sky-phone, eager to communicate with Valon and all nine operators, who had vowed to actively support the success of this shipment.

"Valon, how is everything running at your end?" Armend asked, wanting to make sure his orders were being followed.

"Just as you ordered, Armend," Valon responded, as he sat at the long table in Armend's villa in Tirana. "The 'red dust' was loaded onto the container ship and packed inside the upholstered furniture. Don't worry boss; nobody will ever find it. But there is another problem we can't seem to fix!" Valon said as he examined the list of bank accounts on his laptop.

"What problem?" Armend asked, his heart beginning to beat a little faster.

"Many of our operators aren't receiving their payments! There seems to be a problem with bitcoin deposits during these past few days," Valon said. "Our operators are refusing to continue working for us if they don't receive their payments immediately!" Valon explained, fearing Armend's wrath.

"They will have to complete this operation, or none of them will be paid anything!" Armend shouted into his phone. "The nine operators who came to my meeting vowed to make this shipment a success, and now they have to deliver on their promises!" Armend continued as his blood pressure shot up.

Armend ended the call with Valon and quickly arranged for a video conference call with the nine operators, but only four of them accepted his invitation. He couldn't seem to be able to get through to the other five. The four operators refused to appear by video and only accepted voice communication, which made Armend angrier, even suspicious. The four operators vowed to offer their technical support but wanted an advance payment until the bitcoin debacle was sorted out. Armend tacitly agreed and promised them an extra bonus when he returned safely to Tirana.

An hour later, Armend received a phone call from Valon informing him that Assem had assured Marwan that Port Said was the docking harbor but that Farida had left her apartment sometime during the past 24 hours and never returned. Armend told Valon that Farida was clearly working with the Egyptian police and that he should make sure she paid the price for betraying them.

But then Valon said something that caught Armend completely off guard.

"Armend, Assem also reported that Maged hasn't been to the police station for the past two days and that nobody has heard anything from him," he said, his voice failing to mask his discomfort.

"The Egyptian police have clearly formed some kind of plan, Valon. They are prepared for a showdown with us in the Mediterranean, and I want you to make sure that all our nine operators connect with me via satellite in one hour from now. We have to review our counterattack," Armend said, his adrenaline surging once again. "Assem would never betray us, but clearly Farida and Marwan have. Both have to be punished immediately!" Armend ordered as he clenched his fist.

Armend hung up and began pouring over the satellite images on his laptop, making sure the weather conditions were stable during the coming 48 hours and that no navy or coast guard vessels were visible on his ship's satellite route. The cartel made sure the container ship was equipped with infrared detectors, which would be able to pick up the presence of vessels or any obstacles along the ship's sea lane. Armend had contracted some of the best nautical and marine engineers in Albania to foresee the success of this shipment's delivery, and he was adamant that he would return back to Tirana a victor.

While Armend waited for the operators to contact him, Nora was busy packing a small backpack and getting ready to quietly escape from her mother's house. She could see two of Armend's men watching the house from a distance, but her mind was firmly made up. She was going to leave for her cousin in Serbia. Her cousin told her she had rented a small studio for her and that she had already arranged for Nora to be picked up from a road just two blocks away. Nora was going to escape at four o'clock in the afternoon. She was going to pretend that she was going to the supermarket for some groceries, when in fact she was going to exit the supermarket through the back door. Her cousin told her to quickly get inside the blue Volkswagen that would be parked by the curb.

Nora knew she was risking her life, but she also knew that she had betrayed Armend today. She couldn't trust anyone anymore except her own flesh and blood. Her cousin was the only person she could trust in the whole world now. So, at exactly four o'clock, Nora left her mother's house and headed to the supermarket, which was two blocks away. She entered the supermarket, bought two items in cash, and quickly went out through the exit door, as planned. She spotted the blue Volkswagen parked by the curb and rushed to open the back door. She got inside in a hurry.

"Hello, Nora," the man she had met at the park said, calmly, as he pressed the central lock button. "We promised to keep you safe, and we always keep our word."

Chapter Thirty-Four
'Quantum'

Maged managed to get only three hours of sleep before Rawan and Kamal entered the 'bunker,' carrying two duffle bags. It was four o'clock in the morning, and Maged didn't understand why they had arrived so early. He looked at them quizzically, his red shot eyes blinking rapidly to adjust to the rays of sunlight that briefly streamed in from the outside.

"We have less than 48 hours to complete our mission. Rawan and I received orders to take you to another classified location where we can all see this operation through," Kamal said quickly, as he and Rawan began disinfecting the 'bunker,' carefully wiping off the surfaces with a specific solution, switching off the computer systems, and turning off the electrical generators. Three minutes later, two men dressed in construction worker overalls walked into the basement and began stripping the screens off the walls, folding each screen carefully. Maged watched on as the two men carefully covered each screen with green scaffolding, then transported them outside on a long gurney.

"Will the admiral be joining us at this new location?" Maged asked, looking at Kamal, who seemed unusually alert today.

"He is already there with several other intelligence agents," Rawan answered, as she pulled her heavy sweater around her waist. "He will be coordinating the naval and coast guard operation from a specific control room," she continued, as she began walking toward the door in a hurry. Maged and Kamal followed her out of the 'bunker' and all three headed toward a black van parked right outside the door. Maged's eyes began to slowly adjust to the bright light as they drove off toward the new location.

"Maged, how much longer will Hamed be left to roam around freely? Assem already knows that you've found out about the fingerprints. How will you explain this to your task force?" Kamal asked suddenly, as he gazed outside his window.

"Hamed is under very strict surveillance. He continues to go to work every day as if nothing has happened," Maged said, feeling strapped inside his seat because of the tight seatbelt. "I have been doing nothing for the past two days but trying to piece together all the circumstantial evidence that I have collected about his involvement in the murder. Hamed's fingerprints and hair strands may have been planted in Suite 55 to incriminate him in Mona's murder. Given that he's the housekeeping manager, the fact that his fingerprints were found on the list and on the button does not confirm that he actually killed her," Maged explained, looking toward Kamal.

Kamal and Rawan glanced at each other, as if Maged had just spoken their minds. Maged then noticed that the driver wore dark sunglasses, fitted with some sort of black audio device, and that his face was utterly expressionless as he calmly drove the van.

"Who do you think is the actual killer?" Rawan asked. "It's not really part of my role to ask, but I'm eager to unravel this murder too," she said, as the rain began to hit the windshield.

"There is more than one suspect in my mind," Maged answered back, preferring not to mention specific names at this point.

Maged then looked outside his window, noting how the streets of downtown Cairo were gearing up for New Year's Eve. Several shops had cheerful Christmas decorations hanging across their display windows, along with end-of-the year sales. He watched as people on the streets began to shield their heads, scurrying off in different directions as the rain began to fall harder. The van steadily made its way across the Sixth of October Bridge and all the way into New Cairo. He wondered where they were headed, but based on their location, it seemed like they were heading toward the New Capital.

He was right. The van eventually parked at a construction site two kilometers east of New Cairo. It was a structure with green scaffolding covering its façade. Maged expected to see the same two agents that had guarded the entrance to the 'bunker', but he was wrong on that account. He followed Rawan and Kamal to the back of the structure, where they were met by a big steel entrance. Rawan pulled out a magnetic card and inserted it into a slot. A faint beep was heard, after which a small facial recognition screen slid open. Rawan came as close as she could to the screen, after which the steel entrance opened slightly, allowing only one person at a time to file through.

Once the three of them were inside, Maged was surprised to see at least ten people inside a wide open space, with black ear buds in their ears, each one of them staring at their computer screen. There was so much commotion that Maged was taken aback by how different this location was compared to the one he had just left behind. He began scanning the place, his eyes trying to spot the admiral. He then saw him sitting at a rectangular table, speaking with two other navy officers.

"Welcome to Quantum Headquarters, Officer Maged," Rawan said, projecting the pride she felt. "This is my team's brainchild. A unique state-of-the-art intelligence capsule where the most advanced and experienced quantum engineers meet to solve a multitude of problems, and often to create them," she explained, as she sat at a round table, hurriedly flipping open her laptop.

"This is one of the locations where Rawan and her division have been working for the past ten days to disrupt the 'red dust' cartel's bitcoin blockchain networks. They have been very successful and are waiting for directives to halt the networks completely," Kamal said, as he took a seat at the same table.

"Rawan, as the communication expert in this place, I wanted to ask you if I may check the messages on my phone. I've been afraid to check them since yesterday, fearing that someone from the cartel could be trying to track my location," Maged said, suppressing his constant urge to check his text messages.

Rawan told Maged that it was imperative that he leaves his phone turned off for the coming 48 hours. She told him that the 'Code Red' task force was networking together in full force now to win this satellite communication war and that they couldn't afford any glitches or mishaps.

Just then the admiral walked across to them, asking them to join him quickly in an adjacent chamber where two navy engineers were busy looking at satellite images on their computer screens. They looked up as the admiral walked in, then continued on with their discussion. Maged likened the energy in the Quantum Headquarters to popular sci-fi movies he'd seen on TV, where everyone knew exactly what they were doing and why they were doing it. The admiral then moved toward a large computer screen which was projecting live satellite images from the Mediterranean Sea. Maged could see a few dark shapes move very slowly across the screen. The navy engineers began to zoom into the images, enlarging the dark shapes until they focused on one particular gray shape.

"This is our target," the admiral said, placing his fingers on the enlarged image. "This is the container ship we are targeting. Our intelligence reports now confirm that the cartel's drug lord is aboard this vessel," the Admiral continued.

"Who is he? Where's he from?" Maged asked, with desperation evident in his voice. "This man is the cause of death of at least four people I know of! Can you imagine how many others may have lost their lives because of him?" Maged asked, as anger now took over.

"True! That's exactly why we are cooperating with Interpol to capture him alive," Kamal responded calmly. "Our intelligence agents have managed to convince his girlfriend to testify against him. She's been offered a deal by Interpol, and she has accepted it," he continued.

"His name is Armend Lika, Albanian, living in Tirana. He's been the cartel's drug lord for the past two years. His right-hand man goes by the name of Valon. He has operators all over the Mediterranean region and was aggressively trying to expand his operation into Egypt and North Africa," Rawan explained.

"He has managed to buy the allegiance of Assem, who is his 'lieutenant' in Egypt, besides contracting the service of several hitmen and 'falcons,'" Kamal finished off, lowering his voice so that nobody other than the four of them could hear what he was saying.

"Consider him finished off from this moment onwards," Rawan said. "Our agents here in Quantum are busy tracing and blocking all bitcoin transactions related to this cartel, and in a few hours he will have nobody on his side," she said with confidence.

Maged listened to the information being said, eager to know everything he could about this drug lord. But with less than 35 hours left till the vessel entered Egyptian territorial waters, the one thing on his mind now more than anything else was who to find out who actually killed Mona El Safty. It was his responsibility, and he owed it to Mona. He left the others and sat at a small table on the other end of the chamber. He needed to gather his thoughts and recreate the narrative he had formulated earlier.

He pulled out his pen from his pocket and began to write down his thoughts on a notepad:

'Taking all the evidence found at the scene of the crime into account, there's a high probability that Hamed could be the killer. But I have doubts that he did it. I recall how he encouraged Camillia to tell me what she saw in Suite 55 on the morning Mona's body was discovered.'

'What if Camillia had planted Hamed's shirt button and strands of his hair in Suite 55 herself in an effort to frame him? Could it be possible that Camillia had killed Mona? Can I assume that Camillia worked with the cartel and that she was planning on distributing the drugs found in her bag to local dealers? Was Camillia killed because she messed up Mona's murder so badly? Could she have written the names on the list herself to extort more money from the cartel? Did they kill her to make her pay for double crossing them with the police?'

"Alright everyone, please listen carefully," the admiral said, speaking into a small microphone attached to his headset. "According to the vessel's nautical speed, it will enter Egyptian waters in about 30 hours from now."

"Our agents are about to paralyze the cartel's blockchain networks. The cartel has its own computer engineer and hackers, who will definitely try to counter our communication assault," Rawan continued on, speaking into her headset's microphone, her hair tied back in the usual messy bun.

Maged immediately stopped writing, listening intently as the admiral and Rawan laid out the framework for the impending communication assault as well as the naval interception of the container ship. The plan was worked out with such meticulous precision that Maged wanted nothing more than to watch their plan being executed. The energy inside Quantum Headquarters made Maged feel like he was caught in the eye of the storm.

"Officer Maged, you said you wanted to check your text messages. One of our computer agents will assist you to read them quickly," Rawan said, as she pressed a button on one of the panels. "Don't worry, he will also block your location, just in case the cartel is waiting to know where you are," Rawan said, as she left the chamber.

Maged thanked Rawan and then continued writing his thoughts on the notepad again:

'Could Assem be the killer? He could have used his policeman expertise to obtain Hamed's fingerprints and strands of hair, placed them at the scene of the crime, and then disposed of the body using the staff elevator. I am sure Assem sent Camillia the threatening messages. So doesn't it make sense that he was the one who planted the drugs in her bag to silence her? And what was he doing in Camillia's apartment the night before she was killed? It makes sense that Assem would be the person who was in contact with Mona, posing as some national security agent. He could have been the one who instructed her to go to the Maharaja restaurant the night of her murder.'

"Officer Maged, please hand me your phone," the intelligence agent said, disrupting Maged's train of thought.

Maged gave him his phone and waited for a few minutes as the agent adjusted some settings. Maged then hurriedly began scrolling through his text messages, spotting several messages from members of his task force. He noticed a message sent from an unknown number. He clicked on it. It read:

'If you're reading this, we must thank you for your cooperation. We now know where you are.'

Chapter Thirty-Five
'Plan B'

Armend barely managed to get four hours of sleep after a very tumultuous day. Several of his operators had complained that they hadn't received their bitcoin payment transfers, expressing their desire to leave the 'red dust' cartel in search for more lucrative opportunities. But after much effort and cajoling, Valon managed to convince several cartel operators, most of whom had attended Armend's meeting in Tirana, to fulfill their pledges, and he repeatedly assured them that Armend would compensate them once the shipment was successfully completed.

Armend was mostly agitated because he had tried to call Nora twice to make sure she was alright but her phone was switched off. He asked Valon to check up on her and became even more distressed when the two bodyguards watching her mother's house reported to Valon that she had gone out for grocery shopping but hadn't returned to her mother's house for the past 24 hours.

"Armend, this isn't the time for us to be discussing Nora! I will contact her and make her call you back. Now you must focus on the operation and on your own safety," Valon said, fearing that Armend would lose his concentration.

"Make sure she's alright, Valon. If anything has happened to her, I will know how to get my revenge!" Armend shouted, feeling increasingly claustrophobic inside the small room.

"We are scheduled for a video conference call with several operators in about 15 minutes," Valon said. "Tell them exactly what you want. We only have 24 hours left!" Valon explained, still doubting Armend would be focused enough for the task.

Armend began to tightly clench his fists. With less than 24 hours before the ship entered Egyptian waters, he was beginning to feel like a trapped prey inside the enclosed space, as he began to regret the rash decision he had made to board the container ship. Shortly after, Armend received a request to join the video conference. Only five operators were present in the meeting; the others had refused to partake in the operation without getting an advance payment.

"The five of you will be handsomely rewarded once I'm back in Tirana. That's a pledge I am making to you now. I value your loyalty," Armend said, as he tried to mask the anxiety he was developing inside his gut.

A lump began to form in Armend's throat as he began to experience increasing network glitches with his satellite connectivity. Armend assumed it was because of weather conditions at sea, but he became very suspicious when Valon also reported experiencing unusually weak internet connectivity from the villa in Tirana.

"Valon, leave the villa immediately! They know your location! Get out now!" Armend shouted.

Valon didn't argue. He quickly gathered his laptop, his heavy jacket, and his backpack, almost tripped over the cables and wires on the floor, and dashed toward the entrance. Once outside the villa, he was immediately surrounded by three Interpol officers, one of whom quickly put handcuffs around Valon's wrists while another officer read him his rights. Valon couldn't believe what was happening, but it was too late.

"You are committing a grave mistake! I am not Armend! He is traveling for business! I am just a friend looking after his property while he's away!" Valon shouted, trying to remain loyal to Armend for as long as he could.

"We know who you are, Valon!" said the third officer calmly. "Calm down. You will have a chance to give a complete confession," he said, as they escorted him to a classified location.

Armend continued on with the video conference for another six minutes, oblivious to the fact that Valon had just been arrested. He told the four operators exactly what he wanted them to do during the remaining few hours, after which his satellite connection began lagging, to the extent that he had to end the meeting because the operators were no longer audible. He desperately hoped that Valon had made it out of the villa in time and that he would get back to him with news about Nora.

There was a hard knock on Armend's door.

"Mr. Armend! We are having some satellite connection difficulty, but the navigator promises it will be resolved quickly. He will continue sailing according to plan toward the destination," the deck officer explained, his face showing clear of distress.

Armend began to feel very uneasy now. The fact that Valon's phone was now switched off, coupled with Nora's sudden disappearance, made him suspect the obvious. It was now clear to him that Nora had been arrested by Interpol and that she had confessed against him to save her own skin. He was even angrier that her betrayal cost him the arrest of Valon, his right-hand man. Armend tried to restrain himself from experiencing a full-blown panic attack. He clenched his fists, took three deep breaths, after which he tried to contact his two other assistants.

The connection was very poor, but he managed to get through to one of them.

"Valon is down! Proceed with the plan as fast as you can! Change your current location immediately, then leave Tirana!" Armend ordered.

Armend's door swung open. It was the deck officer again. This time his face showed even signs of full blown panic.

"Mr. Armend, you will have to come with me to the navigation bridge! The captain needs you there! Now!" he said, as he led Armend quickly to the container ship's navigation bridge.

Armend found himself in an area with several display screens adjacent to one another, all beaming live radar images. The captain anxiously looked at Armend as he pointed to one of the screens. Armend watched and listened carefully.

"There are two vessels making their way toward us! I am assuming they are Egyptian navy vessels or coast guard ships, and we have less than eight hours before we enter Egyptian waters. What do you want me to do?" the captain asked, trying to conceal his panic.

"Continue onwards toward our destination! Even if they attempt to intercept this vessel, we have covered our tracks very well. They will not find anything! Our plan is airtight!" Armend said, determined that the 'red dust' shipment made it to the Port of Alexandria.

Armend explained to the captain and deck officer that he had already devised an escape plan for this exact scenario. He told the captain that he wasn't a fool to attempt to embark on such a risky voyage without having a 'plan B' under his belt. While Armend revised his 'plan B' with the captain and deck officer, Maged and the 'Red Dust' taskforce gathered around a large computer screen which was beaming live satellite images of the two navy vessels as they steadily made their way toward the container ship. Maged had already overcome the anonymous text message scare after an intelligence agent hurriedly switched off the phone. Maged quickly alerted Kamal and Rawan as to what had happened to prevent the Quantum Headquarters location from being detected by the cartel's satellite network.

"Maged, we have alerted our agents to comb the area in case any of the cartel's operators were trying to infiltrate our location. We always have a one-kilometer cordoned-off zone around our premises anyway," Rawan had explained, her confident tone calming Maged's growing anxiety.

Feeling confident that Rawan, Kamal, and the Admiral had the operation under tight control, Maged went back to his notepad to continue sifting through his 'murder bytes' in search of the identity of Mona's killer.

'I don't think there is a third possibility as to who the killer could be. It is clear in my mind that it is either Hamed or Assem. Maybe I am complicating the evidence when it could simply be Hamed. It is time to

arrest Hamed and Assem. I can't wait another minute, knowing that Mona's killer is walking the streets freely. Armend already knows that the Egyptian navy is heading toward his vessel. He is watching the operation unfold just as we are here. I have to move now.'

Maged abruptly stopped writing and went to speak to Rawan and Kamal. He told them he was ready to arrest Hamed, Assem, Marwan, and Farida. He believed that either Assem or Hamed could have killed Mona, but that the evidence in his possession pointed squarely to Hamed. As for Assem, Marwan, and Farida, they would all be arrested anyway for working for the cartel, but Farida would get a reduced prison sentence for helping the police expose the drug ring.

"Do you think Assem and Marwan are still in Egypt? They must have escaped somewhere by now," Rawan said, her face giving nothing away as she watched the live satellite images.

"That's not possible because all of them are under strict police surveillance. Look, I have to go back to the *Zamalek* police station and resume my role as head of this task force. It was prudent to stay in classified locations for the past two days, but I can't hide anymore," Maged said, pacing back and forth as he spoke.

"We will have you watched around the clock from the moment you step out of here," Kamal said, as he looked past Maged's head. "And you're right. You have to arrest them. *Inshallah,* we will arrest Armend and bring down the entire cartel. You go get Assem, Hamed, and the others," Kamal said, as he shook Maged's hand and wished him good luck.

Maged left Quantum Headquarters in a black van, escorted by two intelligence agents. They were going to drive him all the way to the *Zamalek* police station, and they informed him that they were ordered to stay with him until the operation was over. Maged looked outside the back seat window, realizing how much he had missed the bustling streets of Cairo, with all its traffic, crowdedness, and diversity. With only a few hours left till New Year's Eve, Maged watched as pedestrians crossed the streets in the familiar end-of-year rush, eager to finish off their errands before the stroke of midnight.

He marveled at ordinary people's excitement with their daily lives and how different his life was from the norm.

Chapter Thirty-Six
'Zero Hundred Hours'

The police station was crowded for this time of night. Maged elbowed his way into his office, and when he asked about Assem's whereabouts, an officer told him that he had just left for Alexandria for New Year's Eve. Maged immediately sent Kamal a text message, expressing to him that either the shipment was going to dock at the Port of Alexandria or that this was one of Assem's decoys to throw off the police. To verify the information, Maged contacted the two officers who were tailing Assem to inquire about his exact location. One of them confirmed that Assem had indeed arrived in Alexandria two hours ago by car and that he was staying at his friend's apartment in the *Sidi Gaber* area.

Maged left the police station and told the two agents to drive him to Alexandria immediately. He had decided to arrest Assem himself, and he didn't want any of the police officers in the station to know anything so that no one would accidentally tip Assem off. Maged felt an inner burn to watch Assem's face as he was being handcuffed, to watch him being handed a heavy prison sentence for being a 'red dust' mole. But more importantly, Maged wanted Assem to pay for betraying the police force and his country. Maged understood that the coming hours would be fraught with danger and risks, but he was willing to put his own life in danger to ensure that the likes of Assem would never have a place in the police force again.

After exactly two hours on the Cairo-Alex road, the black van arrived in *Sidi Gaber*. They parked a block away from the building where Assem was reportedly staying. Maged contacted his officers, ordering them to keep a close watch on Assem and alert him if he left the building.

Meanwhile, Maged headed quickly to the Port of Alexandria in the black van, firmly believing that Armend had already briefed Assem about the two vessels that were headed toward the container ship. Maged was also sure that Armend had already figured out that the Egyptian coast guard and navy would intercept the ship once it was inside Egyptian waters.

Maged called Kamal to get the latest update from Quantum Headquarters.

"Kamal, what's the latest at your end?" Maged asked hurriedly, as he strapped his handgun to his belt.

"The container ship entered Egyptian waters two hours ago, and according to the Admiral's navigation route, it is steering toward the Port of Alexandria! Did they really think we would buy Marwan's story of docking at Port Said?" Kamal asked incredulously. "The admiral is coordinating the course of action now with the coast guard and navy. Armend knows it's only a matter of time before he's arrested."

But Maged wasn't so sure the coming crucial hours would end so predictably. He was certain Armend and the cartel had several alternate scenarios underway to cause maximum collateral damage. He knew he had to move quickly now so that all operators would be arrested with orchestrated precision. He called members of his task force at the *Zamalek* police station, telling them to arrest Hamed, Farida, and Marwan immediately. He knew it was time to bring justice to Mona and Camillia. Maged arrived at the Port of Alexandria, discreetly slipped through the security gate, and told the agents to remain inside the black van, outside the Port's premises, so as not to alert Assem when he arrived.

Meanwhile, realizing that the coast guard was closing in, Armend Lika ordered the captain to quickly reverse course. He knew he had failed the 'red dust' cartel, but all he wanted to do right now was to protect himself and the 'red dust' on board the vessel. He settled for the fact that he had lost the battle for Egypt, but he didn't want to lose the war. He also realized that he was either going to be arrested or he would have to go into hiding in Mersin for quite some time, with the possibility of never returning to Albania. With Interpol now actively hunting him down, he believed that Turkey was the safest hideout for him, given the political unrest that had been burgeoning in Istanbul and Ankara lately. But Armend's order was met with an unexpected response.

"Mr. Armend, I cannot sail back to Mersin without refueling! We are so close to the Port of Alexandria, and the vessels are heading directly toward us! I'm afraid it's too late to change course!" the captain said, frantically watching the green radar signals on the computer screens.

"Prepare a speedboat now!" Armend ordered him, telling him to continue on to the Port of Alexandria, where Assem would know what to do with the 'red dust.'

But it was too late for Armend. Before the Captain could make a decision, two helicopters appeared out of nowhere and began circling above the ship, hovering over them like two motionless lovebirds. Ropes were then thrown down from the two helicopters as eight coast guard soldiers, dressed in heavy protective gear, began to climb down onto the ship's deck. Armend watched in horror as his dreams were being shattered before his very eyes. He suddenly pulled out an army knife from his back pocket and lunged toward the captain, holding him in a chokehold position.

"Take me to the speedboat now! Move it!" Armend screamed at the captain, as he began to drag him by the neck outside the navigation bridge.

The other officers on board watched in terror, as Armend pulled the Captain onto the ship's deck, wielding an army knife in his other hand. But before Armend could get any further, three coastguard soldiers attacked him from behind, freeing the captain from his chokehold and pinning him down on the deck.

"You think it's that easy?" Armend said, his voice muffled by the sheer strength of the officers pinning him down. "You may have captured me, but there are many others who will take over! You'll see!"

Kamal, Rawan, and the admiral watched Armend's arrest play out live on their large computer screen, amidst loud cheers and rounds of loud applause! Rawan thanked her team of computer engineers as well as the entire Quantum Headquarters task force for their diligence and hard work, as Kamal slowly began packing his laptop into his duffle bag. The admiral thanked the two navy engineers for their effort, then walked over to Rawan and Kamal to bid them farewell.

Kamal and the admiral walked out of Quantum Headquarters side by side, escorted by four intelligence agents. They shook hands and parted ways, not knowing if they would ever meet again. But that was the nature of their service to the country. They appeared only when national security issues were at stake. They were the unknown soldiers who fought intelligence wars of the fifth generation. They battled narcotics drug lords, domestic and international terrorists, and anything or anyone who threatened the peace and security of their country.

Kamal pulled out his phone to share the good news with Maged. He wanted to tell him that Armend was arrested and that the 'red dust' shipment was impounded by a joint coast guard and navy operation. He also wanted to tell him that their 'Code Red' task force had succeeded with flying colors. But when he dialed Maged's number, there was no answer. Kamal began to worry that Maged could have been injured in a confrontation with Assem. He called the two agents that were assigned to protect Maged. The agents told him that Maged was inside the Port of Alexandria and that he had given them orders to stay inside the van, outside the premises of the Port.

"What do you mean Maged is inside the port alone? Go inside immediately and give him back-up!" Kamal shouted.

After a 20 minute grueling wait, Kamal received a call from one of the agents who had gone in search of Maged.

"Officer Kamal, I can't find him inside! He's nowhere to be found; I searched everywhere! I asked all the dock workers, and they denied seeing him anywhere!" the agent said, sounding out of breath.

"Put the chief of the Alexandria Port Authority on the phone immediately!" Kamal ordered, as he began to fear the worst.

Kamal explained the urgency of the situation, then asked the chief to playback his CCTV footage of the past hour, and to zoom onto the Port's entrance. The chief did as he was instructed, conveying to Kamal that a man dressed in civilian clothing had indeed snuck into the port exactly 57 minutes ago and that the footage showed him heading toward a cargo room near one of the wharves. Kamal began to worry that Maged may have been ambushed by Assem's 'falcons' and that he was in danger. He immediately called the agents who were tailing Assem and ordered them to storm the apartment where he was reportedly staying.

About 20 minutes later, Kamal received a call confirming that Assem had been arrested, after fiercely denying that he had anything to do with the 'red dust' cartel. When Kamal tried to call Maged again, he still didn't receive a response. At that moment, Kamal got in touch with the intelligence agents in the 'Code Red' taskforce, instructing them to head immediately to the port for a search and rescue operation. The Chief understood that this was a matter of national security, and he proceeded to close off all entry and exit points in an effort to facilitate the search for Maged. But the cold winds and rain made the search effort even more difficult, as word got around that there was a rescue operation for a police officer underway.

It was now past midnight. Outside on the streets, people joyously rang in the New Year as they walked together in close-knit groups, singing, chanting, and laughing out loud, completely oblivious to what was taking place inside the port. Meanwhile, all the storage rooms, cargo handling zones, and toilets were being searched by experienced secret agents and sniffer dogs as the port was transformed into what looked like a crime scene in a movie. Nobody inside the port was permitted to leave, and nobody unaffiliated with the 'Code Red' dragnet was issued security clearance to enter. The port had become a closed cage.

By the crack of dawn, four hours into the search, there was still no sign of Maged, until two agents accompanied by a sniffer dog discovered a small abandoned backpack. There was a wallet inside which had an ID card belonging to Maged. The agents reported the finding to Kamal immediately, who in turn briefed the Minister of Interior. The Minister had been closely monitoring the murder case all along, keeping in close contact with the 'Code Red' taskforce. He ordered Kamal to go to

Alexandria himself to lead the search for Maged and for Hamed to be taken into custody immediately.

Two hours later, Kamal arrived at the Port, and was questioning two port handlers who had seen Maged slip through the security gates shortly before midnight, the night before. They remembered him looking suspicious as he walked briskly toward one of the cargo hangars near the wharf. He kept looking around him as if in fear of being followed by someone. Kamal and his team of agents interrogated every cargo handler on duty that night, none of whom recalled seeing Maged again once he had entered the port.

"Kamal *beh*! Kamal *beh*!" shouted one of the dock workers as he rushed toward him.

"What did you find?" Kamal inquired, his gut suspecting the worst as he watched the man approach him.

"There's a body floating near the wharf, over there!" the dock worker shouted, as he frantically pointed his index finger in the direction of the body.

Kamal felt shattered for a few minutes before he finally managed to regain his composure.

They all ran toward the wharf, expecting to find Maged's body.

Chapter Thirty-Seven
'Fallen, but Never Forgotten'

Maged's body was placed in a wooden casket, which was then covered in the Egyptian flag before being transported in a hearse back to Cairo. Kamal rode in the passenger seat, reading verses from the Quran, as the ominous vehicle made its way along the Alex-Cairo desert road. He tried to control his emotions but failed miserably when tears slowly slipped down his cheeks. He wiped them off and smiled as he remembered Maged's facial expressions, his mannerisms, and the way he would pace back and forth whenever he was deep in thought. He shuddered from the cold weather outside and tried to calm himself down, vowing to give Maged the honorable burial service that he deserved.

But Kamal couldn't understand how Maged was stabbed three times in the back, even though he had always carried a loaded gun. Not finding the gun left him in even greater distress, knowing that a policeman's gun was akin to his badge of honor. He kept walking through several scenarios in his mind to figure out how the killer could have taken down such a well-trained policeman. The only way he could make sense of it was that Maged was walking toward the cargo hangar when he was ambushed by someone who already knew his identity. Someone who expected him to be there. Kamal believed that Maged had committed a fatal mistake when he told the two agents to stay in the car while he slipped into the port alone, without cover. Kamal looked at Maged's backpack, which had been bagged at the port for forensic evidence. He slipped a pair of latex gloves on and slowly opened the bag to examine its contents.

Kamal found Maged's notepad, the one he had been writing his thoughts on at Quantum Headquarters. Kamal read the last page:

'My final conclusion should be that all the physical evidence points to Hamed as the killer. He had access to all the suites on the fifth floor, as well as to the staff elevator. But Camillia had told me that she had found the list halfway under the curtain. Was it placed there intentionally to be found later on by the police? Could Hamed have written that list himself after killing Mona? It is unlikely that a piece of paper could have accidentally fallen from the victim and tucked itself halfway under the curtain, which was made of heavy fabric. But why would Hamed write that list unless he was told to do so? What did Hamed stand to gain?'

'Was Hamed promised something in return? One person on the list vanished; another was killed in an apparent car accident. Two others naively defied the cartel's mandate, while the 'lieutenant' himself was being watched closely and will be arrested shortly now. Was Hamed ordered to write the list so that these five operators would be taken down by the police?'

'Could Mona herself have tucked the list halfway under the curtain? But when did she have the time to do that if her killer was present with her the whole time? Could Hamed have gone to use the toilet, leaving his victim outside on her own? That isn't a realistic scenario to me. His eyes would have been glued to his victim the whole time.'

'Could Hamed be the next 'lieutenant'? But, then, why would Hamed place his own hair in the sink and drop a shirt button at the scene of the crime?'

'What if the actual killer is none of the above?'

That was the last line Maged ever wrote.

Kamal shut the notepad. He called Rawan immediately to follow up on Hamed's arrest.

"Rawan! Was Hamed arrested?" he asked, looking out of the passenger window at the sprawling desert outside, which flanked the two-way road from both sides.

"Yes! He was surprised when our agents went to the hotel to arrest him," she said, as she left Quantum Headquarters to attend Maged's burial service.

Kamal let out a loud sigh of relief. He knew he would be assigned the stressful yet deeply rewarding job of interrogating Hamed and Assem himself. It was his point of strength. He was known in the national security sector to be the one who asked the tough questions, the one with an emotionless poker face as well as the stamina to interrogate suspects, often for hours on end. He never tired, and he always produced results.

The hearse made its way toward the now wet and crowded streets that led to the *Sayidda Nafisa* mosque, where a group of policemen and civilians had already gathered to attend Maged's funeral. Kamal spotted Rawan dressed in heavy black clothing with a black veil wrapped loosely around her head. Kamal noticed that she wore dark sunglasses, probably to watch the people attending the service. He also spotted a number of undercover agents scattered around the premises of the mosque. Kamal always admired how intelligence agents, such as Rawan, were always on the lookout for suspects, for evidence, and for thin threads that often led to big breakthroughs.

Kamal's eyes scanned the area until he saw Maged's father standing outside the mosque's main entrance, accompanied by some male relatives and friends of the fallen policeman. Maged's father was in a state of utter shock and grief as tears ran down his face. Kamal approached him to offer words of solace, applauding Maged's courage and patriotism throughout the investigation.

"God bless Maged's soul. He was a great policeman who took pride in his job and in his country," Kamal said, as he shook the father's hand and patted him on the shoulder.

"Did you see him before he died?" Maged's father asked, his eyes red and watery from all the sadness, the memories, and the tears.

"Yes, I have. He wanted to catch the killer and solve this case. I promise you his wish is my command," Kamal responded, his heart wrenching from the sadness and grief he saw in this man's face.

"But son, I never saw you before! How long have you known Maged, God bless his soul?" the father asked, his expression one of wonder mixed with heartbreak.

"For as long as I should have. Long enough to know the kind of man he was and the lengths he would go for this country," Kamal responded, his voice full of pride.

"Catch his killer! Make my heart rest," the father said, as he squeezed Kamal's hand. "What's your name, my son?" he asked, tears still falling down his grief-stricken face.

"My name is not important, but I promise you justice, *Inshallah*," Kamal said, as he patted him once again on the shoulder, then calmly walked away.

Kamal attended the burial service, then took a taxi to his apartment in *Nasr City*. His wife and two kids greeted him warmly at the door, as they hadn't seen him for the past two weeks. Kamal managed a smile before heading directly to his bedroom, shutting the door quietly behind him. He needed to be left alone for a while before he faced the herculean task of interrogating both Assem and Hamed. He needed to gather all his strength and evidence before this upcoming confrontation. He was now assigned the task of finding both Mona and Maged's killers. One victim was murdered for trying to uncover the truth about the 'red dust' cartel, while the other was murdered for trying to catch her killer.

An hour later, Kamal was dressed and headed to the police station where both Hamed and Assem were locked up, awaiting interrogation. Kamal looked at himself in the bathroom mirror, seeing Maged's face smiling back at him. He smiled back at the mirror, as if reassuring Maged that his killer would pay the ultimate price for his heinous crime.

Half an hour later, Kamal sat across the table from Hamed, who was sweating all over his white shirt. He looked at Kamal with absolute fear in his eyes.

"Hamed, the trusted Imperial Hotel Housekeeping Manager. How much did those bastards pay you to kill Mona?" Kamal asked calmly, as he looked somewhere above Hamed's head.

"I didn't do anything!" Hamed pleaded. "You have the wrong man! I encouraged Camillia, God bless her soul, to tell Officer Maged everything she saw the morning of the murder!" Hamed said, as he held his head in his palms.

"Do you know your hair was found in the sink, in Suite 55? Your shirt button was also found on the floor. Why did you do it, Hamed?" Kamal asked, his adrenaline kicking in now.

"They framed me! I check the suites every day for cleanliness! They know it's my job, and they framed me!" Hamed shouted, banging the table with his fist.

After a full hour of continuous questioning, Kamal asked the guards to take Hamed back to his cell. He then asked them to bring Assem in.

"What did Armend promise you, Assem? You were already his 'lieutenant' here. Were you promised to become the drug lord of Egypt?" Kamal asked, enjoying the shock on Assem's face when he heard Armend's name being mentioned.

"Armend? I don't know who you're talking about," he calmly said, using his own police interrogation prowess to control his emotions and body language.

"Really? Listen to your own voice then!" Kamal said, as he played back recordings of Assem's conversations with operators from the 'red dust' cartel. "Do you know the price of betraying your police badge? Of betraying the trust of the people? Isn't the police department's slogan, 'service to the people?'" Kamal asked, as he slowly turned up the heat on Assem.

"Of course! That's exactly why I did what I had to do to bring Mona's killer to justice," Assem said, his voice steady.

"Justice? You betrayed Maged, your fellow policeman! You had him killed, just like you killed Mona! And Camillia! The 'red dust' capsules were found in your apartment, Assem. We have recordings of Marwan and Farida discussing your explicit role in operating and facilitating the 'red dust' cartel's operations in Egypt. You exploited your police connections. Oh! Did I mention that we also have you on camera too?

Why did you kill Mona, Assem? Did she not agree to your demands? So, you had to frame Hamed for it?" Kamal asked as he looked at Assem straight in the eye.

"What evidence do you have that I killed Mona? Or Maged, God bless his soul? Or Camillia? Camillia's killer is in prison now. Go ask him! Even if you have evidence that I work for the cartel, you have nothing on me in those killings," Assem said, as he realized that he wouldn't be able to deny his affiliation with the cartel due to the overwhelming amount of evidence against him.

"Tell me why, and how, you got them killed, Assem. If you confess, we will consider sparing you the death penalty. You'll get life in prison with hard labor instead," Kamal said calmly, as he looked at the neon track lights on the ceiling.

"What guarantees can you give me that I will be spared the death penalty?" Assem asked, realizing the noose was getting tighter around his neck.

"The likes of you deserve no guarantees. Confess or face the consequences," Kamal responded calmly.

After two hours of continuous questioning, Assem eventually told Kamal all the details that he wanted to know about the killings and the 'red dust' cartel's operations in Egypt. He told Kamal that he didn't know the identity of Mona's killer, but that he was probably a foreign operator contracted by the cartel. He did admit, however, to contracting the sniper who had shot and killed Camillia. He eventually also admitted to contracting the hitman who stabbed and killed Maged at the port.

"How did you know Maged would go to the port?" Kamal had asked.

"I knew I was being watched. I also understood that Maged had already figured out my role in all this. Valon, the drug lord's right-hand man, wanted Maged out of the way in order to secure the New Year shipment. I also understood that Farida and Marwan were meeting and that Farida had sold me out to save her own skin. I had Maged tailed, just as he had me watched," Assem had confessed.

Kamal walked out of the interrogation room, letting out a loud sigh of relief, as national security agents patted him on the back and congratulated him for extracting the confession. He drove directly to Maged's father, whose apartment was about 30 minutes away. He walked up to the door and rang the doorbell, waiting impatiently for the door to swing open.

"It's you! So soon!" Maged's father said, his eyes swollen from all the crying and emotional anguish.

"I promised you that we would capture Maged's killer. I'm here to tell you that we delivered on that promise," Kamal said, his heart full of pride.

"Really? That's the best piece of news! Thank you, *Allah*! My son's death has been avenged!" the father cried out, holding his head in his hands and sobbing loudly.

Kamal patted the old man on the shoulder and quietly walked out of the apartment.

Epilogue

Maged's killer was later identified as Hamada El-Abyad, an Egyptian drug dealer and mobster with a long rap sheet of drug dealing convictions and prison sentence evasions. The presiding judge handed him the death penalty. It was swiftly served on February 21, 2020.

Mona's killer was later identified as Emir Ruslan, a Turkish-Albanian acquaintance of the murder victim. He was immediately arrested by Interpol in Luxembourg and is currently serving his life sentence in a classified location.

Kamal and Rawan continue to serve their country with pride and honor. These are not their real names.